# Lioness:

# Mahlah's

Jou

Barbara M. Britton

This is a work of fiction. Names, characters, places, and incidents either are the product of the author's imagination or are used fictitiously, and any resemblance to actual persons living or dead, business establishments, events, or locales, is entirely coincidental.

**Lioness: Mahlah's Journey**
**COPYRIGHT 2019 by Barbara M. Britton**

Contact Information: titleadmin@pelicanbookgroup.com

All scripture quotations, unless otherwise indicated, are taken from the Holy Bible, New International Version(R), NIV(R), Copyright 1973, 1978, 1984, 2011 by Biblica, Inc.™ Used by permission of Zondervan. All rights reserved worldwide. www.zondervan.com

Cover Art by *Nicola Martinez*

Harbourlight Books, a division of Pelican Ventures, LLC
www.pelicanbookgroup.com PO Box 1738 *Aztec, NM * 87410

Harbourlight Books sail and mast logo is a trademark of Pelican Ventures, LLC

Publishing History
First Harbourlight Edition, 2019
Paperback Edition ISBN 978-1-5223-0253-7
Electronic Edition ISBN 978-1-5223-0225-4
**Published in the United States of America**

# *Dedication*

To my sister Tove, and my sisters-in-law Sherrie and
Suzanne. Women who go forth with God.

# Acknowledgements

This book would not have been possible without the help of so many people. My family has been the best cheering section throughout my publishing career. I am blessed to have their love, encouragement, and support.

A big thank you goes to my editor, Fay Lamb, who helped make the daughters of Zelophehad shine. I am also blessed to have Nicola Martinez in my publishing corner. She has brought all my stories to light through her leadership at Pelican Book Group.

My fellow Coffee Break leader, Brenda Fennema, mentioned the daughters of Zelophehad at our leaders' meeting, and the story came to life in my mind. I'm glad Brenda shared the story of these brave girls, so I could share it with you.

The author communities of WisRWA, ACFW, RWA, SCBWI and my publisher Pelican Book Group, have been a huge support in my writing career. The Barnes & Noble Brainstormers keep my word counts thriving every week along with my Mo's Crew champions. Thank you.

My church family has kept me going during good times and bad. What a blessing to have their loving support.

And last, but not least, The Lord God Almighty, for giving me the gift of creativity and breath each day to write these stories. I am a cancer survivor, and not a day goes by that I don't praise the Lord for his healing. To God be the glory.

# The Daughters of Zelophehad

Mahlah
Noah
Hoglah
Milcah
Tirzah

*The Tribes of Israel from Numbers 26:*

Reuben
Simeon
Gad
Judah
Issachar
Zebulun
Manasseh, firstborn of Joseph
Ephraim, son of Joseph
Benjamin
Dan
Asher
Naphtali
Levi, no inheritance of land

*Books by Barbara M. Britton*

*Tribes of Israel Series*

Providence: Hannah's Journey
Building Benjamin: Naomi's Journey
Jerusalem Rising: Adah's Journey

*Daughters of Zelophehad*

Lioness: Mahlah's Journey
Heavenly Lights: Noah's Journey
Claiming Canaan: Milcah's Journey

# A Prior Journey

After the Hebrew people fled slavery in Egypt, they wandered in a desert wilderness for forty years until it was time to take possession of God's Promised Land. Passing through Moab, the Israelites now camp across the Jordan River from the fortress of Jericho and wait to conquer their inheritance.

At last, the battles begin...

# 1

*Charm is deceptive, and beauty is fleeting;*
*but a woman who fears the Lord is to be praised.*
*Proverbs 31:30*

Mahlah arched her back. A sky, blue and crisp like a faceted gem, draped over the camp. No trade winds cooled the warmth of the fresh, new sun. She picked up a basket from outside her family's ramskin tent and wedged it against her hip. Grasping her woven belt, she shifted the leather, so her knife was but a flinch away. She wouldn't allow any beast in the wilderness to harm her sisters.

"Come on, Tirzah. The dew is gone."

Tirzah emerged from behind the tent flap. She blinked at the brightness and wrinkled her nose. "Why do I have to gather manna?"

"Because it is your turn." Mahlah reached to take the hand of her youngest sister. "Hurry now, before Father stirs."

A gurgling noise rumbled from Tirzah's belly.

Mahlah stifled a laugh. "We better go before your hunger wakes the neighbors."

"It won't." Tirzah pressed her lips together. Her stone-collecting satchel hung at her side.

"If we stay here and let our kin harvest the closest

manna, your rumble will turn into a roar." Bending low, Mahlah lunged forward and wrapped an arm around her sister. She lifted Tirzah off the ground and twirled her in the direction of the outskirts. "Manna awaits."

Tirzah giggled. A few sleepy gatherers scowled and clutched their unfilled baskets.

The tent flap flung open. Zelophehad stomped into the small clearing outside their dwelling.

Stiffening, Mahlah faced her father. Heat crept from her neck into her cheeks. She lowered her sister to the trampled path.

Tirzah pressed her weight against the folds of Mahlah's robe.

"Enough of this silliness." Her father glowered at her empty basket. "How can I oversee a brood of girls on an empty stomach?"

"I'm sorry we disturbed you, Father." Mahlah's heartbeat pounded in her throat. "We won't take long."

Head down, Mahlah tugged her sister toward the next tent. Nothing she did of late pleased her father.

Tirzah jogged a few steps. "Are we breaking camp today?"

"We'll see from the hill."

Mahlah hurried Tirzah past row after row of ram-skin tents occupied by their tribesmen of Manasseh. The sour scent of the hides filled her nostrils as she hastened toward the fields bordering their camp.

A few women chatted in hushed voices. They, too, needed to collect a day's worth of God's provision this morn.

"I'm tired of the desert." Tirzah scuffed her sandals along the dirt path separating their clan of

Hepher from other families within the tribe of Manasseh.

"Shhh." Mahlah glanced to see if any of the women had heard her sister's complaint. Not one head turned. Praise be for sleepy neighbors.

"I am weary, too, little one, but someday soon we will have a house to keep and land to farm. You can tend the livestock or weave our garments."

Tirzah puckered her cracked lips. Her eyes grew wide. "I'd rather cook."

"Ah." Mahlah chuckled. "May God grant me the remembrance of your volunteering for labor."

The desert outside the encampment opened into an expanse of nothingness. The soil and hills and bramble bushes were muted shades of nutshells.

Layers of manna rested on the parched grass. This bread of heaven came in the morning while quail came at night. These provisions were bestowed by their God. The God of Abraham, the God of Isaac, and the God of Jacob.

*Shalom, Adonai.* Mahlah stooped to break off pieces of the thin, bumpy bread. With four sisters to feed and an aging father, no complaint would leave her mouth about the lack of variety in God's gift. Every finely ground tidbit tasted of fire-roasted grain. She accepted the nourishment with pleasure.

"Do we have honey at home?" Tirzah nibbled a piece of the unleavened bread. Her satchel bulged from her labors.

Mahlah nodded. *Home.* The word sounded strange, as if spoken in a foreign dialect. For the last five years, they had traveled without a mother. A mother who had made their tent a refuge in the desert. On the providence of God, their family moved from

3

place to place. At times, the marching seemed aimless. And aimless is what her father's direction had become.

Leaving Tirzah at the base of a hill, Mahlah climbed higher and shaded her eyes to survey the camp. Tent upon tent formed a perfect square with the Tabernacle of God set in the center of the tribes of Israel. A cloud hovered over the sacred site. No marching would be done today. Only waiting. Would the rest heal her father's weariness?

Mahlah gripped her basket and hurried down the slope. Her sandals skidded on loosened pebbles. She left the small stones embedded in her toes, and hurried, hoping her father had not grown impatient. She prayed a full stomach would breed acceptance of their wandering.

"We have enough, little one." Mahlah tapped Tirzah's shoulder and trudged ahead. "Let's go."

Tirzah gripped her satchel as if a thief might snatch it away. "Slow down. Your legs are longer than mine."

"Only for a while with as fast as you're growing." Mahlah hurried toward their family's tent.

Tirzah hopped behind her, one footstep to the other, as her manna-filled satchel beat a rhythm against her hip.

Mahlah shook her head at the drumbeat her sister created and grinned. "I will volunteer to eat your manna crumbs."

Her father rounded the far side of their tent. "Where is my food?" His words pierced the morning calm, drawing the attention of nearby kin. He overturned a water jug. "Again, we have nothing to drink."

Every muscle in Mahlah's arms tensed. Her

knuckles ached as she gripped the handle of her basket. She slowed her pace. Her mind searched for an excuse as Tirzah slammed into the back of her legs. Sweat pooled above Mahlah's lip. With one swipe of her tongue, she removed the moisture but tasted salt and grit.

What could she say to calm her father's ire so his temper did not draw another reprimand from the elders? She stepped forward, her progress hindered by Tirzah's grasp.

*God give me wisdom.*

"I'm sure our goats have been milked. Isn't milk more satisfying than water?" She tried to smile, but her lips quivered.

"Babble!" Their father hurled the stone jar at the ground.

Mahlah flinched. Shards of baked clay decorated the dirt. Her sisters, Hoglah and Milcah, stood in the tent opening, eyes wide and mouths gaping as if they'd encountered an evil spirit.

"You are a fool if you think there is enough to drink. We will wither away like your mother." Pacing in a circle, their father ripped his turban from his head. "Don't offer me that awful bread."

"Father, please." *Forgive him, Lord.* Mahlah handed her basket to Tirzah and pushed her younger sister nearer the tent.

"Moses has cursed us all," her father shouted. "Do you see a bountiful land? What bounty can I claim with no heir?"

Fisting her hands, Mahlah strode toward her father. Hadn't she worked beside her father and done everything an heir could?

"We are blessed. With life." Her head covering

shifted to one side, but she would not stop to right it. "I beg of you. Go inside and eat. I will send Tirzah to fetch some milk."

Nemuel, an elder from the tribe of Manasseh, stomped into the open space between the tents. His son, Reuben, lagged, towering over his father.

Her father slipped off his belt and whipped it high. "Moses must answer for our hardship. Who believes as I do?"

Mahlah bit down on her lip. Her family did not need another tongue-lashing from a leader. Her father's discontent would draw another public reprimand. Nemuel showed no compassion toward his kin, but perhaps Reuben would remember favorably the girls growing up in the tent a few paces from his own.

She stepped closer to her father and feigned lightheartedness. "Hunger has made you like a bear." She grinned as if they attended a celebratory feast. "Come and eat with your girls."

A few men approached the clearing. Had they heard the commotion?

"Zelophehad." Nemuel crossed his arms, splaying the tassels on his garment. "Repent of this grumbling and see to your daughters."

Swinging his belt high as if harvesting wheat with a sickle, her father remained silent.

Nemuel backed away.

Elders retreated.

A tiny spasm twitched in the corner of Mahlah's right eye. She blinked, trying to calm the flutter. Why now eye? She needed to take heed of her father's actions.

"Lead the way to justice, Zelophehad," a man

yelled from a neighboring tent.

"No." Mahlah pointed at the heckler. She drew to her full height and fingered the blade on her belt. How dare this sluggard threaten her family?

"Be still," she said. The spasm in her eye tugged at her cheek.

Her father snapped his belt inches from her toes.

Mahlah's heart raced, but she did not retreat. She swallowed the lingering taste of fine grain and swept moisture from her eye. "*Abba*." She croaked her plea. "Let us sup as a family." She indicated her sisters huddled outside the tent. "Follow me inside."

She did not recognize the snarl of the madman beholding her with eyes as dark as a moonless midnight. Where was the loving father who had laughed at his daughters' antics?

"It is time I take my grievance to the Tabernacle." Her father strode toward the center of the camp while holding his belt aloft like a scepter. "Moses must answer for my misery."

Men from the tribe of Manasseh marched after their wayward clansman.

"Father, wait." Why wasn't he listening?

"Repent of this wickedness," Reuben called out, echoing his father's wisdom. "God's wrath will find you."

Should she follow her father? She glimpsed her youngest sisters, Tirzah and Milcah, sobbing into their older sister's apron. Didn't their father care about the future of his offspring? Life would be uncertain for women with no protector and no heir.

"What is wrong with you people?" Nemuel chastised the onlookers as he shuffled in the direction of another leader's dwelling. "You stand and gossip and ignore the Lord's gift? Gather your manna before the sun is too high."

Shrill screams came from the direction of Nemuel's tent. Were others angry with God?

She scanned the wide path angling by their neighbors' tents and toward their place of worship.

Reuben's young son, Jonah, raced toward his father. His tiny arms stretched for an embrace. Reuben's stoic composure crumbled. He bent low to catch his son.

Mahlah sprinted forward. "Are you hurt, Jonah?"

The boy changed direction and wrapped his arms around Mahlah's knees, nearly knocking her to the ground.

She steadied herself and gave Jonah a hug. Tears flooded the raven-haired boy's eyes. Eyes as dark and thick-lashed as his father's. Had the shouting and arguments upset the three-year-old?

"Shalom, now." Mahlah picked up the small boy and breathed in the soap scent on his skin. His small chest rose and fell like the sea. Would her father be calmed if a son greeted him like this every morning? If only her father had a son. "Why are you crying?"

The boy turned his head side to side. Was he looking for something or someone?

Reuben tried to coax Jonah to leave her arms. "If he has set his mind on a task, my mother cannot move fast enough to catch him."

*As the wife you recently buried.* She silently finished what went unspoken in Reuben's troubled gaze.

Jonah placed his hands on Mahlah's cheeks and squeezed. She could hardly talk with Reuben about her father's behavior while her lips imitated a fish. She shook her head to loosen Jonah's grasp.

More screams wakened the camp. This time they came from the east and from the west.

Reuben turned toward the Tabernacle.

She glanced in the direction from which Jonah had run. The dirt path moved. She blinked, but the soil still quaked in her vision.

Her skin tingled from toe to scalp. Hardened ground didn't tremble. She blinked again.

No mistake.

One. Two. Three.

Three snakes slithered toward her toes.

# 2

"Reuben, watch your feet." Mahlah dipped her head toward the sidewinding intruders. A shiver shot through her body leaving a trail of bumps across her skin.

With a slight hop, Reuben drew nearer to his son. He stomped on the ground, arms flailing, to deter the snakes from coming closer.

The serpents veered toward cries in a nearby tent as if drawn by the panic.

She slouched and brought Jonah higher on her hip, all the while watching where she stepped. "Look how brave your father is, Jonah."

At her praise, the boy reached for Reuben and practically leapt onto his back. Reuben turned in time to grasp his son.

Shrieks pierced the cramped space near her family's tent, and Mahlah whirled around. Two asps slithered toward the opened flap.

Twelve-year-old Milcah almost knocked over her older sister, Hoglah, as she scrambled to get away. Tirzah hurled the basket of manna at the ugly pair of slithering beasts. Manna scattered on top of the dirt as ribbon-like bodies intertwined into a ball.

One snake was not uncommon, but five in such a short span of time?

Where was her father when she had need of him?

Mahlah's thoughts sobered. Her father had insulted Moses, loudly, among their clansmen. To curse their leader and God's provision had proven deadly before. Then, the ground had split and swallowed the blasphemers. Now, the ground beneath her feet crawled with venomous snakes.

She cast a glance at the asps. Untangled, they renewed their assault on her ramskin home.

The mellow taste of manna turned to vomit in her throat.

"God of Jacob, defend my family." Her petition joined the numerous voices rising from the camp. Stomping closer to the basket Tirzah had thrown, Mahlah unsheathed her blade. She gripped the basket's woven handle and used it as a battering ram to deter the asps.

One enemy retreated. One hesitated and readied to strike.

Heat surged through Mahlah's battle-ready body. How dare this cursed serpent attack a daughter of Manasseh?

The bold asp, mouth unhinged, struck her direction. Mahlah pushed off with her thighs and let the tension in her muscles unleash as she backhanded her knife. The snake's head dropped to the soil and lay like a partially crushed grape.

She shivered as the rest of the corpse crumpled to the dirt.

"Sister, come inside." Hoglah held the tent flap open.

Mahlah kept her blade waist high. She scanned the soil. Where were Reuben and Jonah? Her heart sagged. A father had to protect his child. Shouldn't her father have protected his children?

She hurried into the tent and closed the flap, tight.

Tirzah cradled a large piece of granite in her hand. Milcah inspected the seams of the ramskin. Tiny dots of sunlight adorned her face. If a weakness was to be found, her keen sense would spy it out. Hoglah stood statue still, arms crossed, hands rubbing her skin.

"Has anyone grumbled against God?" Mahlah's voice sounded more desperate than her father's. "Tell me now. I beg of you." Tears threatened to spill, but she would not shed a single drop. She willed her weak eye to remain steadfast. How had a routine morning become a nightmare? "Milcah?"

Milcah shook her thin drape of brown hair. "No, I wouldn't."

"Mother never did." Hoglah stopped patting her arms. "She taught us not to speak against God."

"Father complained." Tirzah held up her rock and let it rest on her small shoulder. "I heard him when we came back from the hill." Her eyes bulged. "Were my words bad?"

Mahlah's heartbeat almost drowned out the thud of leather sandals slapping the paths outside their tent. Tirzah didn't lie. Their father had disregarded an elder of their tribe and caused an uproar. Were the snakes a punishment for his insult of Moses? Of God?

Mahlah shook her head. "You were a tired child, Tirzah. Whining about your duties is not challenging God. You enjoyed God's food, didn't you?"

Tirzah nodded.

"Father's grown weary." Mahlah swallowed hard so her words came out in a comforting tone and not harsh with condemnation. How else could she explain her father's chastisement? "We serve a just God, but I must find Father and insist he repent of his insults. If Father asks God's forgiveness, God will be merciful."

"You're leaving us?" her sisters chorused.

"Stay inside the tent, and you will be fine." She truly believed her words, but sensing her sisters' fear, she held out her arms. "Come here, and I will pray for you. For us, the daughters of Zelophehad."

"What about Noah?" Milcah wrapped a piece of hair around her finger.

What about Noah? Knowing their sister, she would not leave her livestock and herds even in a poisonous snake invasion. Mahlah's chest tightened at the thought of being in the open fields with serpents lurking near every stone. *Oh Lord, protect Noah. I need her.*

Mahlah stroked Milcah's hair. "Jeremiah is with her. His staff is no match for any asp."

A smile graced her timid sister's face. Mahlah cherished the hint of a grin in all this madness.

Tirzah shuffled into the center of the circle. "I was grumpy about the manna. Will I get bitten?"

"Not if I can help it." Mahlah kissed Tirzah's forehead.

Holding all her sisters close, for a moment, lest a snake wiggle under the folds of their tent, she prayed, "Hear our plea, O God. Keep us safe this day. Watch over our father and sister and our people. Forgive us if our lips spoke against you."

"Let it be so," Hoglah whispered, her fingers trembling.

Drawing Hoglah into her chest, Mahlah smelled a waft of cinnamon. Why couldn't honey and spices on manna soothe their father's unrest? Her middle sister tried so hard with so little to make meals a delicacy.

"Now, watch over each other." Mahlah let go of her sisters and opened the tent flap. She waited, knife at the ready. One heart race. Two. No onslaught of snakes bore down on their threshold.

She dashed outside and ordered her sisters to lace the tent.

Mahlah charged from her home, past the rows of tribal tents, toward the center of camp. Voices clamored inside and outside the nomadic homes. She scoured the path for any sudden movements. Every so often, a loud wail would rise above the dull rumblings of her people. Had fangs found flesh?

As she passed an elder's tent, a man rounded the front lead. He stumbled over the tent stake and collided into her side. The stench of moldy goats' milk filled her nostrils. She grabbed hold of his garment to steady herself.

"Run!" the man screamed. "God is judging us."

If God was judging the tribes of Jacob, where was the man going to hide? They were surrounded by rows of ramskin.

The man ripped free from her grasp.

Knocked backward, Mahlah swung her arms. She gripped an overhang by the entrance to the tent to remain upright.

"*Toda raba*," she mocked.

A serpent slid along the smooth-skinned roof, its eyes intent on her face. It hung within striking distance, flicking a tongue between two fangs.

Her heartbeat boomed in her ears, but she didn't move a single muscle.

Men and women ran by without a glance at the sculpture of a woman staring at two tiny onyx beads engorged with her reflection.

Pulse hammering in her temples, she challenged the snake.

"I serve Adonai." She prayed her truth rang out because her throat was dry as a desert stone.

Silence. Stillness.

The snake trembled. Was it getting ready to strike?

She leaned away. How quickly could she dash to the main path?

The serpent plummeted from its ramskin ledge. Straight down. Dead.

Mahlah ran. She dodged bodies lying in the dirt with swollen faces and purple lips. Loved ones cried out in mourning. Children whimpered, their cheeks streaked with tears. Others chanted prayers amidst the *thwack* of swords and branches beating defiant snakes.

"God help us," she shrieked, as if God stood an arm's length away. "Help me."

She sprinted into the clearing, around the vibrant-linen Tabernacle wall and headed east to the gate. Moses would be by the gate. He had to be. He would know how to stop the attack.

Nearing Moses' dwelling, bile rose in her parched throat. Her mouth stung as she swallowed. Men and women writhed in pain. Corpses formed a half-moon around the opening to the Tabernacle courtyard.

Mahlah pulled her head covering across her face. If only the cloth and her hair could shut out the moaning, weeping, and stench of urine.

Where was her father? How could he be so irresponsible to chastise God? He had five girls to oversee. Noah and Hoglah could entertain a betrothal request, but Milcah and Tirzah were too young. They needed a father. An overseer for their family.

"Zelophehad," she called. "Son of Hepher."

She tugged her veil below her chin. Pungent wafts of death assaulted her nostrils.

Moving slowly among the mourners, she beheld the bodies.

"Who is here of Manasseh?" Anyone? She passed a woman who lay face up, an asp coiled on her belly.

"Over there," a man said. He pointed with an arm scarlet and swollen. "Repent of your sins. Moses is bringing a cure."

"Praise be to the God of Abraham, Isaac, and Jacob." She gave a head bob toward her kinsman. God had heard her prayer. A cure from their leader Moses would end the suffering.

Mahlah weaved her way among the people, some sitting, some raising arms toward Moses' tent. She scanned the landscape for snakes but did not see another slithering culprit.

Glancing to the left, she halted. Her body trembled. "No!" Swift as a lion, she ran, dropped to her knees, and skidded toward her father. He lay on his side. His hands were the size of melons and almost as round. Bubbles amassed on his plumped lips. Was he breathing?

"Father, it's me, Mahlah." She grabbed hold of what once was a normal hand. Her father's flesh was cool even though the sun radiated overhead.

"I'm here now." She forced a smile, tears streaming down her face. "Don't leave me. Don't leave us."

His gaze traveled toward her but no recognition showed in the rich-brown orbs.

"Moses is bringing a cure. I will stay here and comfort you." As she stroked his cheek, saliva wet her fingers. "Hold on. It won't be long."

A small group of men marched along the linen wall of the Tabernacle. With tears welling in her eyes, the scarlet, blue, and purple threads in the boundary tapestry blurred into a rainbow of color. Moses led the band of men. He held a bronze-colored pole with the image of a snake at its tip.

"Gaze upon the snake," Moses shouted. "Heed my words." His command filled the area where the injured and dead amassed. "You must look up to be saved of your transgressions."

Mahlah leapt to her feet. She pointed at the healing image. "Father, you must stare at Moses' snake."

Her father did not move.

She knelt and shoved her father onto his back, rolling him onto his other side so that he faced the gate. Moses stood on a wooden box and held the bronze carving high. The amber-colored serpent reflected bursts of sunlight. Mahlah blinked at the intense glare.

"Look up." Her words rushed forth. "Do you see the serpent?"

Nothing. Not even a twitch came from her father's body.

"Father?" She held her hand in front of his nose. Breath. Faint. Praise be.

Bending low, she made sure her eyes were even with his. "Abba, we need you. I need you. Do not leave me. You are the leader of our family." Even with her lips quivering, she remembered the love her father had bestowed at times and blessed him with a brave-hearted smile.

Moses stomped toward her. "God will forgive your insults. Lift up your stiff necks." He waved the pole back and forth above the carnage.

Her body quaked. She didn't know when it began,

and, try as she may, she couldn't stop the tremors. Her father was not casting the smallest glance at the bronze-sculpted snake. She grabbed hold of his beard and hair and tried to tilt his chin.

"Moses is walking away. Come on, Father." She tugged his head backward. "Look up. Who but you will take on five daughters?" With a firm hand, she patted the side of his face. "We have to get our land. Our promised land."

"Mah-laaah." Her father's quiet rasp stabbed at her heart.

"Father? I'm here, Father." His head grew heavy in her hands.

She kissed his cheek. Gently. Furiously. "Look, Father. Please, look up."

His eyelids drooped.

Resting his face upon the soil, she leapt to her feet. Waving her hands, she screamed, "Over here, Moses. Come back. We need the snake."

Her father's gaze did not shift upward, or downward, or follow her screams.

"Father?"

No response came forth.

She slumped to the ground, not caring if an asp waited. Moses approached carrying the bronze snake. Was it too late?

Wrapping her hand in her veil, she touched her father's body. It grew cold. Stiff to her touch. No more breaths puffed from his nostrils.

"No, God. No."

Moses passed to her right. He held the bronze snake aloft.

Her father couldn't gaze at the sculpture. He had never lifted his eyes.

From the depths of her belly, she wailed.

# 3

Mahlah unfurled her head covering and placed the edge over her father's face. She lengthened the rest of the cloth, so it covered most of her father's tortured body. She was careful not to touch him barehanded, lest she be deemed unclean. Her sisters needed her inside the camp, not ostracized outside the tents. Her tears dripped onto her patterned veil. Moses still wandered among her people with his bronze serpent giving life to those near death. To those who wanted to live. Her father had chosen to die.

Beyond the linen fence, stitched bright and bold, a cloud covered the roof of the Tabernacle. God's presence was through the gate. Yards away. In a haze of fiery white wisps.

"Why God? Why did my father not seek you?" She talked to the cloud as though expecting an answer.

A woman stumbled over a nearby corpse, spilling water onto Zelophehad's feet. The stranger's eyes became wide as plums.

"Forgive me," the woman said.

Mahlah almost burst forth in a crazed laugh. Not because of whimsy, but because the life she knew hours ago had ended. She glimpsed the puddle of water at her father's feet. God had provided cleansing water. Of course, He had. When had God not provided for His people? Hadn't she and Tirzah collected God's bread this morn?

Needless. Her father's death was needless. And careless. Her father had left a seventeen-year-old girl to fend for the future of his children.

"Shalom." The woman hesitated, hefting her jar on her hip.

"Yes, of course, peace," Mahlah mumbled.

Resting on her side not far from her father, Mahlah wrestled with thoughts of what was and what could have been. "God what am I going to do? My sisters are waiting in a tent for their father to come home. What shall I tell them? Shall I hide the truth?" She closed her eyes as her right pupil threatened a twitch.

"Mahlah."

The soft rasp of her name startled her.

She opened her eyes.

Reuben's handsome face beheld her with concern. Had she fallen asleep? Her father's stiff form lay beside her in the dirt. His death hadn't been a dream. His death had been a nightmare. Still was.

Around her, only a few bodies and mourners remained near the Tabernacle. Men from the tribes of Issachar and Zebulun unstaked their tents. Ramskins lilted or lay flush with the ground.

She swept her tongue along her teeth, hoping to moisten her mouth. Her gums tasted like flax.

"Reuben." Her voice cracked as if she still slumbered. "What is happening? I must see to my father's burial."

"The elders of Manasseh will see to our fallen. The cloud has lifted from our meeting place. We must be ready to travel."

Reuben cast a glance at her father's corpse as if

21

seeing it for the first time. "I'm sorry about your father. I wish I would have done more to ease his sorrow."

"You were getting over your own sorrows." She, too, had to overcome the grief of watching the man she loved wed another and begin a family. That was in the past. She had to remain in the present. "My sisters." Her chest constricted. "I have to tell them about our father."

"They are unharmed and unbitten because of your wisdom." Reuben bent low. "Go to them, and know the elders of our clan will watch over you. I am here for you as well."

Was he? What time did he have for five girls? She would take care of her sisters. Hadn't she overseen them since her mother's death? She had done what her mother had asked of her. She had vowed to watch over her sisters. Always.

She clasped her hands together and squeezed. The slight ache in her joints helped her focus on her new reality.

"My sisters and I are grateful, but you have responsibilities to your parents and this tribe, not to mention, Jonah. He needs a father. My father's burdens are on my shoulders now."

Rising by her own might, she turned toward home. Why linger by the husk of Zelophehad? Nothing could be done to help her father now. He had abandoned her and his other daughters.

"Wait." Reuben stomped after her. He came alongside, matching her stride for stride. "The leaders of our tribe will take care of you and your sisters."

Where were her father's relatives when she was the one receiving his wrath? Why didn't they try to intervene and keep him from storming Moses' tent?

She didn't need their oversight. She had been doing fine on her own, until today.

"Do not worry." She kept her tone civil, but it was not kind. "I've had years to learn what a man does." *And does not do.* "I can raise a tent and lower one."

Reuben shook his head. "There's more."

Of which she was well-aware. But at this moment, her loyalty rested with a promise she had made to a dying mother. A promise that she and her sisters would prosper together in the new land. A promise her father had abandoned in choosing death.

"I'm not afraid of my responsibilities, Reuben. I'm the firstborn of my father, and I've worked hard to make this clan proud of our name."

The concern in his gaze clawed at a tiny piece of her heart. She craved a companion as rugged and caring as Reuben, but she would never confess that need. For it was wise to keep that secret hidden away among so many land-hungry kin.

"My family will assist you. We can join our tents." Reuben meant well, but she could never accept his offer while her lungs held breath. "My sister is comforting yours."

"They know?" Mahlah almost choked on her words. With one last glance at her father's body, she darted like a skylark toward home, leaping over anything in her path. Holding her sheathed knife to her hip, she calculated each step and turn toward her tent.

Reuben was ignorant if he thought his sister was a help. Basemath was…was…*Forgive, my thoughts, Lord.*

Reuben's sister saw to her own needs before she saw to the needs of others. How different she and Reuben were, yet they came from the same mother and father. And their father, Nemuel, knew how to wield his power in the tribe and in the camp.

Storming down the path through the tents of her clansmen, Mahlah hurried to aid her sisters. "God of Abraham, may the elders of Manasseh and my father's kin find me worthy to lead." How could they be blind to her skills in managing his household?

Clinks of hammers on tent pegs rung in her ears. A donkey brayed, protesting his new load. Curses bellowed from near her tent.

She passed Reuben's dwelling. But where was hers? Half taken down, the ramskin walls lay folded in the dirt.

Milcah sat cross-legged by a standing wall, head in her hands. The drape of her dark-brown hair blocked the view of her face.

Basemath swung a satchel at Tirzah. "Stop this insult at once."

Arm over her head, Tirzah readied to hurl something from her fist.

More than likely, it was a rock. And more than likely, it was headed Basemath's direction.

"Listen to me for once." Hoglah attempted to keep their little sister from scoring a victory.

Mahlah strode between her sisters and Basemath. "What is going on here? My family is in mourning and our home is a mess." She made sure the rumble of her question reached the next path.

"She." Basemath pointed at a scowling-faced Tirzah. "She attacked me."

"For no reason?"

With Basemath, there was always a reason.

"That is unlikely," Mahlah said.

"Hah! I came to give comfort at my brother's urging, and this is what I receive." Basemath held out her arm and displayed scarlet marks.

"Comfort?" Chin up, Milcah cast an accusatory stare at their cousin. "You told us we were going to be your servants."

Mahlah fisted her hands. She couldn't let abuse go unpunished, but the daughters of Zelophehad would not be serving anyone. Least of all their haughty neighbor, Basemath.

"Do something, Mahlah. Or I will report this to my father." Hands on hips, Basemath kicked a rock at Tirzah.

Had stones already been thrown? Would Basemath twist this altercation into an insult of Nemuel's authority? Or Reuben's?

The clunks of mallets pulsed through Mahlah's temples. A wave, hot and heavy, rolled from her stomach to her scalp. She whipped around.

"Stop taking down my tent." She marched to where her clansmen worked. "Go back to your homes. Can we not have one moment to grieve?"

Wide-eyed, one of the laborers dropped his mallet. "We have orders."

"And I am ordering you to leave." Her voice broke. "Please."

At that moment, the crack of a whip struck near the tent. Mahlah jumped. She placed a hand on her chest to keep her heart from bursting through her tunic.

Whip aimed high, there stood Noah. Cheeks scarlet, brown eyes bearing down on the workers, her squinty-eyed intensity almost scared Mahlah.

"You heard my sister. We will pack our own tent." Noah's beauty turned rabid.

Tools dropped to the ground. Men fled. Basemath

cowered.

Tirzah danced in a circle. Her tear-stained cheeks plumped from her grin.

Mahlah embraced their shepherdess. "Shalom, Noah. To think I was worried about you handling a few snakes."

# 4

Mahlah held her sixteen-year-old sister close. Noah's head covering radiated the heat of the sun and warmed Mahlah's cheek. "My heart rejoices that you are here now. I wished to warn you about the snakes, but I thought it best to go after Father."

"Then the rumors of rebellion are true?" Noah stepped backward and secured her whip. "Another shepherd told me our clan led the rioters." Her dark eyes grew somber. "I didn't want to believe it."

"'Tis true. Father took his temper and insults to Moses." Mahlah swept a tear from her face. "He is no more."

Noah's chest sank to her belt. She tapped her fingers to her lips. "I did not believe he would act upon his utterances." She blinked. "I thought his harshness was for our ears."

"Your whole family is out of control. Rocks and whips." Basemath stomped toward Mahlah. Rolling up her sleeve, she displayed the few small scratches. "My father will hear of this insult. I came at his urging to offer comfort to you and your sisters, and I was attacked."

"By what?" Noah crossed her arms. Leather bracelets covered both of her wrists. "A sparrow?"

Giggles filled the small clearing.

Not one sputter left Mahlah's lips. She needed the support of Basemath's father and brother. "I appreciate your father's concern, but I will see to the well-being of my sisters."

"On whose authority?" Basemath showed little compassion.

Noah rotated her whip. "Mahlah is the firstborn of Zelophehad."

Basemath took a step backward. All the while, she jabbed a finger at Mahlah's face. "How can you lead a family? You are a woman with no husband. No one has even offered a marriage betrothal."

Could this troublemaker shout that truth any louder?

"Someone will seek her. In time." Noah seemed so sure of what Mahlah was not.

Her neighbor barked out a laugh. "Not for a long time. Not after your father brought punishment on our tribe and others. Don't you want Moses to bestow a blessing on our clan? Come under my father's tent and all will be forgotten. He will offer a bride price for your sisters."

"And what will we do under your father's tent?" Mahlah breathed deep and kept her feet firmly planted lest she lunge at Basemath. "Serve you and anyone your father deems worthy?" Her chest heaved. "Shall we forget we are the daughters of Zelophehad?" Her eyes welled to the brim at the mention of her father's name.

"What name do you want remembered?" Basemath opened her arm in the direction of two curious gawkers. "Nemuel or Zelophehad? The living or the dead?"

"Zelophehad," Noah shouted. Her glare glistened

with grief, but it challenged anyone to defy her.

"Enough." Mahlah would not allow her father to be maligned or for Basemath to stir trouble. "Our father was not the first to challenge God, and he won't be the last." Sweat trickled down Mahlah's hairline. She brushed all the wetness into her sunbaked locks.

"Tirzah should ask forgiveness." Hoglah gripped Tirzah's arm like a vice. "Settle this matter in the family before we cause another disruption."

An odd humming filled Mahlah's ears. How could Hoglah side with their squawking neighbor? Hadn't they suffered enough humiliation this day? Where did Hoglah's allegiance lie? And where were her tears?

"We have work to do." Mahlah's throat cinched as she glimpsed an elderly man ordering his family about. Her own father would be left to rot in the desert he loathed. She ran her hand over her uncovered head. "Return to your family, Basemath. I'm sure your mother could use your assistance. I will decide what is best for our sister. We need to tend to our own belongings and finish with our tent."

Down the path, a tent collapsed with a gush of wind. Dust clouded the air as men and women packed their belongings on a donkey and camels.

"I am not going anywhere. I am the daughter of Nemuel." Basemath bared her arm and held it up for all to see. "I demand retribution for this injury." She strutted closer. Her breath breezed against Mahlah's nose. "If you are the head of this family, then bring that brat over here so I can dig my fingernails into her arm."

Mahlah's feet almost lifted from the path. A rush of blood surged through her body. Oh, how she wished to blow the stench of Basemath's words into her slit-eyed face.

"Don't do it, sister." Noah stepped forward. "She is a cold-hearted goat. Tirzah doesn't even reach her hip. Shall our sister suffer more abuse after the loss of her father?"

Glancing sideways, Mahlah beheld her silent youngest sister. She couldn't remember a time Tirzah lacked words. Her sister's tiny fist opened and released a pebble. Her palm was as scarlet as her eyes.

Hoglah did not twitch a muscle. Was she challenging Noah or embarrassed by this confrontation?

"A true leader wouldn't allow this disregard for authority." Basemath cocked her veiled head and smirked. "But then, like father like daughter."

Specks of light blurred Mahlah's vision, but she had worse problems than her own insult. Noah's wrath threatened to lash out at their accuser. Mahlah straight-armed her sister and pushed her toward the tent.

"I will answer her challenge," Mahlah said, "as the oldest."

Noah's ample chest rose and fell under Mahlah's forearm.

"Do not let her break us apart," Mahlah warned.

Noah met Mahlah's gaze and gave a slight nod.

Mahlah whirled around and thrust her bared arm forward. "You want retribution? Then as the firstborn of Zelophehad's daughters, you may take it upon my arm."

"Don't, Mahlah." Tirzah's small body contorted as she struggled against Hoglah's firm grip.

Grinning, Basemath strolled forward and grasped Mahlah's arm. "I'll accept your offer."

Mahlah beheld Basemath's glee-filled stare. She

would have sworn she had seen more warmth in the onyx eyes of the snakes. Mahlah lifted her sleeve. "Let it not be said we are in your debt."

Basemath dug her talon-like nails into Mahlah's flesh.

Tingles. Burn. And then fire. Mahlah's right eye twitched. Of all the times to have a spasm. This was the worst. She clenched her teeth and blinked away any hint of a cry.

Five curved lines grew scarlet and marred Mahlah's sun-browned skin.

"You have lost your standing in this clan," Basemath whispered with a grin born of celebration. "Do not mock me or my father."

Mahlah balled her fist and yanked her arm from her relative's clutches. "I am still the oldest daughter of Zelophehad, son of Hepher. I will see to my sisters' care."

"For now." Basemath scowled in Tirzah's direction and then sauntered toward of her tent.

A trumpet wailed in the distance. The long, low blast urged the tribes into formation.

"Hear that sisters?" Mahlah lowered her sleeve to cover the scratches on her arm. "It is time to pack up our home. We will continue to travel as a family."

A pair of thin arms wrapped around Mahlah's waist. Always-observant Milcah burrowed into Mahlah's side. Her thin body trembled. "I don't want to live with anyone else."

Tirzah hugged on Mahlah's hip and sobbed. "Me neither."

Tears streamed from Mahlah's eyes. This time, it was not because of her twitch or grief. She adored the rough-skin touch of her sisters and inhaling the faint scent of myrtle wafting from their hair. She held out her arms for Noah and Hoglah to join the group embrace. Their father was gone, but his daughters remained, and together they would stay.

Unless.

Unless Basemath had overheard discussions among the leaders of her tribe. Was Nemuel going to separate her sisters? Basemath's words echoed in her ears. They were together for now. Mahlah wouldn't let anyone take her sisters. She had a vow to uphold.

Arms open wide, Noah joined her sisters in a sorrow-filled hug.

Hoglah picked up a tent peg and retreated from her family. "We've work to do since you scared off our kin."

"Yes, we do."

Couldn't Hoglah offer some comfort? Mahlah's stomach clenched. She squeezed Noah and her young sisters tighter before withdrawing herself from their arms. "Now, pack up. We will follow God wherever He moves us." She blew out a strangled breath. "And we will follow God together."

# 5

Hours later, Mahlah stood on tiptoe and squinted at the mass of people following Moses. Dust shrouded the air, but the cloud of their God whitewashed the sky and led the way toward the plains of Moab. Their clan traveled ahead in the distance. She and her sisters lagged at the rear of the tribe of Manasseh, far behind their clan of Hepher. Somehow, she and her sisters had to march faster and keep their relatives in sight. They did not need an overseer. She could manage her family and their livestock, but the tribe at their heels, the tribe of Asher, threatened to overwhelm her sisters, and drag them farther from their kinsmen.

Milcah pulled the donkeys carrying their tent. Another donkey nudged Hoglah's shoulder as it carried Tirzah and the household goods. Noah herded the livestock with another clansman and Jeremiah, the shepherd. At least one member of their clan cared about orphans burdened with heavy hearts.

"When is it my turn to ride?" Milcah shuffled her feet and let her donkeys lumber ahead encasing her between their bellies. "Will we camp soon?"

"We have several hours of sunlight left." Mahlah took the leads from Milcah. "And we need to keep pace with Nemuel's camels."

Tirzah swung her well-rested legs. "They should

wait for us."

"We do not need to be watched over like newborns." Mahlah glanced at the neighboring marchers to see if anyone had overheard their banter. No heads turned toward her sisters.

"I'm not grumbling." Hoglah patted the neck of her beast. "But we are going farther into the wilderness. Is not Moab north of here?"

Like father, like daughter. Mahlah didn't need any reports whispered to the leaders about disgruntled women. Especially women without an older brother or a father.

"We are following our God and honoring the refusal of the leaders of Edom to let us travel through their lands." Mahlah was quick to drown any dissent. "Shall we go to battle with the children of Jacob's brother and fight people of a common ancestor?" She did not want to think of war. War meant sending sons into battle. What brother or son could she offer?

"Why did God give us land with people living in it?" Milcah slumped against Mahlah's hip. "Couldn't He give them another home? Then this walking would be over."

Mahlah shook her head. "All the land belongs to God. It is His to give and take away. But I'm sure He will honor our choice of peace."

"He has given us water for our journey." Tirzah raised her arms toward the sky and pumped her fists. "Spring up, oh well. Spring up, up, up."

"Make her stop," Hoglah muttered. "My ears are tired."

"Who does not like music?" Mahlah held in a rebuke of Hoglah's nagging. "We are blessed to hear singing and not more wailing."

She approached Hoglah while dragging the leg Milcah clung to and used as a bed mat.

"Take charge of all the mules. I will check on Noah." She handed the leads to Hoglah and bent low. "Spring up on my back, Milcah. We will lope around our flocks and help our shepherdess."

"Sure, carry her while I lead these beasts." Hoglah snapped the leather. The harsh crack rang out like another rebuke.

Mahlah pressed out an encouraging smile. "I would carry us all if I could, but I don't wish to sink into the soil."

Playing the mule to Milcah, Mahlah trotted past several families. As far as eyes could see, the hills, valleys, and flatlands were alive with movement. God's people blanketed the terrain, marching in order. Four rows, three tribes in each row, with Levites intermingled, caused a mighty display of strength.

Traveling on the outskirts of their tribe, she spied Noah holding two tiny kids in her arms. The newborns' tongues licked Noah's sleeves. Sheep huddled close by waiting for Noah to give direction.

Noah standing idle was an uncommon sight. Something must be wrong.

"Hold on." Mahlah dashed through bleating sheep and obnoxious head-butting goats. The odor of warm, musty animal hair filled her nostrils. She plodded closer. "What's wrong, sister?"

Noah juggled the babes in her arms. "My mother is gone. I need her to nurse. She has never wandered off." Her dark lashes fluttered. "I have to find her."

Milcah's weight bore down on Mahlah's shoulders. The herds had to keep moving. Each minute they stood on the outskirts talking, their clan journeyed farther north.

"Where is Jeremiah?" Perhaps he had the mother. He and Noah knew each other's animals as their own. The young man couldn't hear or speak, but his herds flourished under his ardent care.

"He has the rest of our sheep. I told him to go on so his father wouldn't complain." Noah blew out a long breath. "I've never lost a goat. Not a single one."

"Find Jeremiah. Stay with him near our sisters. Milcah and I will search for the mother." She jiggled her shoulders. "Right, Milcah?"

"I go where you go."

Noah hesitated. Hand shading her eyes, she scanned the landscape. "How does a nursing animal go missing?"

"Go on," Mahlah urged. "I will pray to God, and He will show me where to find our goat."

*Maaaah.* The kids in Noah's arms agreed.

"I am sorry, sister. I was intent on not losing our sheep. I do not know what happened to the mother." Noah nodded toward the ground. "Take one of the waterskins. I don't need you in distress."

"The mother couldn't have gone far. We will catch her in a blink." Mahlah bent her knees and dipped to pick up a waterskin.

Noah jostled the baby goats and hurried off, her hips swaying among the swarm of stoic wanderers.

Milcah pointed in the distance. "If I was going to hide, I'd sneak behind those rocks."

Beyond the numerous mounds of dirt, a plateau rose from the rolling burlap-colored desert.

"That formation is a long way off for a nursing mother to wander. Her teats would drag on the ground halfway there." Mahlah squinted at the bustle of people intent on spying a spooked animal. Nothing caught her eye.

She grabbed her sister's arms and released their grip. Milcah slid down to the ground. Leading Milcah from the shuffle of herds and herdsmen, Mahlah knelt to pray.

"God of Abraham, guide me to our lost goat. May we be fleet of foot and reunited with our sisters soon."

"Soon," Milcah echoed, with an accompanying sigh.

Mahlah stood and rubbed a hand across her forehead. She stuffed sweat-drenched strands of hair under her head covering. Could the mother have made it to the rocks? She was nowhere in sight.

Securing the waterskin to her hip, she turned to Milcah. "Race you to the plateau."

"Told you." Milcah raised her eyebrows and ran like a gazelle.

Mahlah followed her sister. At an all-out sprint, she dodged a few shepherds and headed toward the rocks.

For the briefest of moments, with her feet pounding the gritty ground and her veil fluttering in the breeze, Mahlah let the angst of the day gust away.

Milcah's spindly legs were no match for Mahlah's thick thighs, strengthened from assisting their father with the tents and waterskins. Passing her sister, she dashed into the thin slice of shade cast by the plateau. She rounded a corner of jagged rock and halted. Her toes dug into the dirt as she pitched forward. The waterskin slipped to her ankles.

Her goat lay on its side, legs bound. A soft bleat rasped from its mouth.

A stranger, draped in a long, embellished cloak,

stood beside the panicked mother.

The man's eyes widened at Mahlah's arrival.

Milcah slid a few feet in the loose dirt. She remained still as a carved sculpture while her gaze shifted from Mahlah to the man and then back again. Not a single word escaped from her pressed-thin lips.

Mahlah's heart beat a *rat-a-tat-tat* faster than a joyous tambourine. She balled her fists at this affront. To the goat. To her family. To her leadership.

Hands on her hips, she shouted, "Let her go. That's my mother."

# 6

Rolling her shoulders, Mahlah broadened her chest and added height to her stature. Noah hadn't lost their goat. This stranger had stolen the mother. But how had he done it among all the herdsmen? Had he targeted them because their shepherd was a woman? Did he know of their mourning? A fiery heat surged through Mahlah's limbs.

An ordinary thief in need of food would be dressed in a threadbare tunic or a tattered cloak, but this foreigner wore garments adorned with crimson and purple thread. Woven in the linen were forms resembling bulls. Oils slicked his hair and bared his gold-banded ears. His fingers and neck glistened with more jewels than she and her sisters owned. Why would a man steal a nursing goat when loosening a ring from his finger would fetch him a feast? Every nerve in her body coiled taut.

"That is my goat." Mahlah spoke with certainty, foregoing a greeting. This fool had separated her from her family and wasted precious time. Time she did not have to waste. "My newborns are crying to be fed. Release her before my father finds us."

She flashed Milcah a side-eye command to let the threat of their father stand.

The thief puckered his lips and stared at her as if

he knew what she had spoken was a falsehood. She had never seen eyes a mix of mustard and amber hues. Truth be told, she had never seen anything like this man. A gust of wind breezed through her bones and sent a chill along her spine.

*God of Abraham, protect us.*

"You are daughters of Jacob. I have seen your tents from the rock." The thief spoke as though he knew their family. "The land can barely hold your people."

A rhythmic thrumming pulsed in Mahlah's ears. She did not have all afternoon to converse with this stranger. What if he was waiting for a band of men?

She lowered her stare from his distracting eyes. "I am a daughter of Jacob and my kinsmen are numerous. Untie my goat so its offspring can nurse."

"From teats round and red?" His cackle made her want to vomit all over his thick leather sandals.

Her knife sat heavy upon her hip. She eased her hand closer to her weapon.

He clasped his bejeweled hands. "You are a lioness. Do you wish to devour me?" He grinned displaying teeth as sharp as her blade.

Mad. This stranger was mad, and she was creeping into madness deciphering his words and watching her goat be tortured by his ropes.

Stepping closer to Milcah and the edge of the jutting rock, she positioned herself to protect her sister, or grab her arm, and run. She took a deep breath. Her mouth tasted of days-old manna.

"Release. My. Goat."

The thief watched her, grinning with those talon-sharp teeth. Light sparkled from the rubies sewn onto his cloak. The red gemstones resembled blood seeping from the dark embroidery.

Milcah shrieked. The long-winded wail nearly burst Mahlah's eardrum. But she would endure the torture to get back to her sisters and to the safety of her people, sooner rather than later.

The thief covered his ears and cursed.

Wind gusted around the rock. Milcah stumbled at its force. Mahlah bent her knees and grabbed hold of her head covering lest it fly into the next city. Dirt and dust swirled in the air. The howl of wind joined her sister's screams. Mahlah's eyes stung. She blinked, trying to keep the bandit in sight.

His cloak fluttered in the wind. More blackened shapes, animal shapes, became visible on his robe. The adorned cloth enveloped his features.

Then, he vanished.

Her skin tingled as if bits of sand sunk deep into her pores. Where had he gone?

Squinting, she whirled around to face a sneak attack. She unsheathed her blade and held it at the ready.

The thief was nowhere in the stone alcove.

*Toda raba, Adonai.*

As soon as the prayer left her lips, the wind calmed.

Milcah back-stepped toward the open desert. "Is he gone?"

"Keep watch while I untie our goat." Mahlah sheathed her weapon and handed Milcah the waterskin.

She ran and knelt beside the mother goat and fumbled with the ropes. She flexed her fingers, willing them to become nimble. The faster they returned to their family and left this rock, the better.

Flinging the rope to the ground, she lifted the mother to her feet.

"Aren't you going to take the rope for a lead?" Milcah kicked at the loose coils.

"No. I don't want to remember that man or possess his belongings. I'm ill from the way he looked at me."

"You? What about the way he looked at me?"

Mahlah shuddered. What was it about that stranger? He made her want to flee this place and never return. *Remember that thief, Lord.*

She cradled their goat in her arms. Poor animal. Its whole body trembled from being restrained.

"Stay on my heels, sister."

As Mahlah hurried from the alcove, warm milk seeped from the frightened mother's teats and soaked her robe. A few drops from the overflowing udders sprayed Milcah's arm. Her once weary sister matched Mahlah stride for stride.

Milcah tapped Mahlah's arm. "We need to find Noah, so the babes can nurse."

"Yes, but we need to hurry." Mahlah chose an easy gait so she wouldn't spook the mother and drench herself further. A wide swath of black and speckled livestock trampled the terrain.

"The tribe of Asher is in sight. Our tribe is farther ahead."

Mahlah's arms blazed with an internal fire. Basemath's scratch marks itched from the pressure of the goat's belly. How she held the mother with muscles she barely controlled was a miracle.

As her people followed God's lead, children scrambled to catch siblings, livestock lumbered under their loads, and an ever-present dust shrouded distant landmarks. The rhythm of sandals slapping hardened ground rumbled louder than a furious thunderstorm.

"Do you see them?" Milcah's sandals dragged in the dirt.

*God of Abraham, help me find my sisters.*

Mahlah propelled herself forward. One step. Then another. Then another.

Sweat pooled upon her upper lip until the crevices in her face became tiny cisterns. Hair clung to her mouth.

"Look for something familiar," Mahlah mumbled.

Her young sister dashed ahead. "I see Noah."

A faded scarlet sling hung from their shepherdess. A newborn goat's head stretched to peer from its side.

When she glimpsed Tirzah holding court atop their donkey, a pressure built behind her eyes. Her sisters had done what she had asked and stayed together. She lifted her eyes to the heavens. "I sing your praise, Adonai."

The load Mahlah carried for being the firstborn of her father lightened as if she had sprouted wings. A reunion was in sight. She giggled with glee as she staggered nearer her sisters.

Noah corralled a few sheep while her sling cradled a babe. A young man held the other boisterous kid. Mahlah did not recognize the shepherd standing alongside Noah. She also did not recognize the man leading Tirzah's mount, or the camel carrying their tent. How had these changes come to pass?

Approaching their shepherdess, Mahlah tipped her disheveled head covering toward the unknown shepherd. "Our family has grown since I left."

"You found my mother." Noah reached for her exhausted goat and petted her neck. "Bless you,

Mahlah. The cries of her young are trying my patience and everyone's in our midst." Noah turned toward her companion. His gaze adored Noah uninterrupted. "This is Shuni of Asher. He and his brother have kept us on the move."

"I see." Mahlah nodded toward Shuni. "I am grateful." Was she? Would these brothers expect something for their labors?

The mother goat wiggled with a fierce determination to escape and feed her young.

"We must let the mother nurse, and then we must catch our clan." Mahlah traipsed to a nearby acacia tree, which made a natural barrier to protect her from the progression of her people. The shade of a thick branch cooled the air heated by the mass of bodies and livestock traveling in the same direction.

Huddled by the trunk, the mother stood and allowed her babies to suck and lap their fill.

Mahlah's belly spasmed. More than one thing had gone right today. She had rescued a portion of their herd. God had protected her and Milcah, too. Her sisters heaped praise on Milcah's notice of the rocky plateau. Mahlah shook the image of that odd thief from her mind.

"Daughters of Zelophehad."

The summons jerked Mahlah into the present and attracted the attention of nearby families.

Elders from her tribe of Manasseh, Nemuel and Abishua, emerged from behind the ware-laden camels and donkeys of the tribe of Asher. Nemuel grabbed hold of the lead to Hoglah's newly gotten camel.

"Whose camel is this?"

"It belongs to me," the brother answered, his grip on the rope unyielding.

Abishua came alongside his fellow leader. "We can take care of these women."

"Apparently not," Shuni's brother said. "Were you planning on leaving them among foreigners?"

Mahlah charged forward. She could not let these men believe she was incapable of overseeing her sisters. If only she did not reek of soured milk and her hair did not resemble a bramble bush.

"Our goat was lost, but now she is found." Mahlah raised her voice and forced a satisfied smile as if she were welcoming the elders to a feast. "We will keep pace with our clan once the mother has nursed."

She nodded to Shuni. "Now that I have returned, I can see to my sisters. May God bless your kindness two-fold." She bobbed her head toward Shuni's brother.

Crossing his arms, Nemuel scowled at her. "Fortunately for you, we are setting up camp."

Praise be. Tonight, she would sleep for hours. "The cloud of God has settled then?"

"If it were that simple, woman." Nemuel clicked his tongue and turned his attention to the young men. "Sihon, king of the Amorites, has denied us passage and stands ready for battle. We go to war."

*We?* The declaration might as well have been an insult. Zelophehad did not have any sons to send into battle. Daughters could not defend the tribes of Israel.

# 7

As night fell, Mahlah hammered the last tent peg into place. War? Hadn't her people seen enough of death in their wandering? What would be said of the line of Zelophehad since they had no warrior to send into battle?

Nemuel and Abishua had treated her like a lost child in front of other men. No respect had been shown to her as the firstborn of her father's lineage. What was to become of a family that did not have a son who could spill enemy blood? How could they inherit conquered land?

She brought her mallet down for one last strike.

Noah trudged closer. The mother goat hobbled at her side. The kids followed their mother's lead in earnest. "If you hammer that peg any harder it will disappear into the earth."

"Better this peg incurs my wrath than others." Mahlah stood. "Forgive my harshness. I cannot bear to be treated like Nemuel's servant. Are we not descendants of Joseph, former ruler of all Egypt?"

"We are." Noah pressed her lips together and let out a sigh. "I guess this is not a good time for me to ask you to help care for our goats. I can't ask Jeremiah to mind them. His father made a fuss about me interfering with his tasks. Is it my fault our flocks are fertile?"

"And you believe Abishua might make this into something?" Mahlah tapped the mallet head into her palm. Why were ordinary concerns weighing on her like millstones?

"Men trade favors all the time." Noah tugged her hem from a curious kid's mouth. "Ask any shepherd and they will tell you I have cared for their sick ewes more than anyone. Our goat limps, and I cannot stay with her and let the sheep wander far."

Mahlah scooped one hungry kid. "I will take them into the tent with me."

"Really?" Noah bit her lip. "Father would never allow it."

"No, he would not. But I do not want another visit from our elders." Mahlah jiggled her hammer to herd the mother toward the tent flap. "I have already found our goat once today."

"Hoglah can herd them inside the tent," Noah said. "I will return after I check on our herds."

"If it were only that easy. Hoglah has grumbled about her responsibilities more than anyone lately. Besides, I don't believe there is an open eye to be found inside."

Noah inspected the mother's stiff leg. "Life will be easier once we get our land."

"It cannot come too soon."

Mahlah grasped the goat's belly and nudged the tent flap with her shoulder. Her sisters, asleep on their mats, did not move a limb to assist her. The mother teetered inside with her young close behind. Mahlah dragged jars and baskets to create a corral for their goats. She unfurled her mat and reinforced the enclosure, so the nesting ground couldn't be easily breeched.

"Lord, give us rest."

The mother goat bobbed her head as if she agreed with Mahlah's plea.

Reaching over the lopsided pen, Mahlah rubbed the mother's nose. "It is tiring taking care of others, isn't it? At least, I do not have to feed my sisters. God has seen to that need."

In an instant, gasps invaded the peacefulness of the tent. Milcah thrashed. Frantic whines escaped from her lips.

Rushing to her side, Mahlah smoothed her hair.

"Shhh. You are safe," Mahlah whispered. "You're dreaming."

Milcah's eyes flew opened. She bolted into a sitting position, breaths fleeing her chest.

"He's coming for me."

"Who?" Mahlah hugged her sister. Was she dreaming of their father returning from the grave? Or—

"That thief. He was chasing me." Milcah's body trembled as she burrowed into Mahlah's chest.

"Do not worry. He was so afraid of us, he fled." Mahlah wrapped her arms tight around her sister. "We will never see him again. And if we do, our kinsmen will protect us."

"He had blood on his feet." Milcah's words rumbled into Mahlah's robe.

"In your dream?"

"No, by the rock. I saw blood stains."

Mahlah envisioned the craggy alcove, the thief's sneer, and his obsession with their goat, but her focus had stayed on the man's chest and arms, lest he lunge in her direction. She had ignored the state of his feet.

"I didn't see any blood." She stroked Milcah's long, soft hair. "Perhaps he stubbed his toe, or better yet, our goat stepped on it."

Even with her comforting words, Milcah's body stayed stiff. Mahlah drew back and stared into her sister's face. Milcah's brown eyes glistened in the lamplight.

"What does God say about stealing?" Mahlah asked.

"That we shouldn't." Milcah's voice grew emboldened as she answered.

"Yes, and God heard our prayers and gave us back our goat. He watched over us, just as he will watch over us tonight." Mahlah smiled reassuringly. "I've brought the goats inside with us, so everyone is safe."

Milcah hesitated. She cast a glance at Hoglah and Tirzah's resting bodies and stared at the mismatched barricade Mahlah had built.

"Where will you lie?" Milcah asked.

"In front of the tent flap so no one will join us. But I must lace it first." Mahlah freed herself from her sister's embrace. "You must sleep, for I pray this battle is swift, and we are on the move once more. When we get our land, all this marching will be done."

Nodding, Milcah settled back down on her mat.

"I love you, Mahlah."

Her sister's wisp of a confession caused Mahlah's heart to ache and then blossom. She could not remember the last time she had heard those words.

Swallowing the lump in her throat, she whispered, "I love you, too."

Mahlah turned and scooted toward the tent flap to secure their dwelling for the night. She reached and took hold of the ramskin.

As she did, a man's rough hand took hold of hers.

# 8

Stifling a scream, Mahlah yanked her arm free from the assailant. Not wanting any stranger to enter her tent, she leapt outside. Hand on her blade, she whipped around ready to confront her attacker and shout for her kinsmen. A warning hung on her lips.

Reuben jumped backward. His mouth gaped.

His dark-eyed, dark-lashed gaze made her heart boom all the way to her belly. He'd always had that effect on her until his wedding day when she hid behind her father and vomited into an empty vessel.

Hand to pulsing chest, she stumbled forward. "Reuben, I almost called a curse upon you, not to mention I could have summoned the whole camp." She paced a few steps to calm her frantic heart and restore some of the energy that had dashed from her body. The slightest trade wind threatened to tip her over.

"Forgive me." He stood immobile watching her blow out breaths as if she had run a race. "I would have sought you sooner, but Moses called the leaders together for a council."

"It must be important." But no one from her tribe or clan had deemed it necessary to include her in the meeting with Moses.

"It is." He straightened to his full height. "I have been chosen to fight for Manasseh against the Amorite soldiers."

"I see." His announcement made her bones weary. The thought of losing another relative troubled her soul. Reuben was not like her other kin; he hadn't spoken one foul word about her father. Not one disrespectful remark in all their growing up years or after her father's shameful death. "What about Jonah?"

"That's why I'm here." He ambled closer. Close enough for her to smell the scent of his freshly washed linen. "If I should die—"

"Folly! Don't speak as such."

He jerked at her response.

"I mean, you will return." She rubbed a chill from her arms. A dam of tears built behind her face, which caused her right eye to flutter. "God will grant us possession of the land. You will return and be greeted with honor."

"It's my time away that causes me worry. My mother is feeble, and Basemath hasn't taken an interest in raising my son." He glanced at his tent as if expecting Jonah to come running down the path.

"If truth be told, your sister's only interest is in herself." Mahlah had the scars to prove it.

Reuben's clenched-jaw grin made her love him a tiny bit more. Being the eldest children, she and Reuben had overseen their siblings for years.

"Jonah feels at home in your tent." He cocked his head toward the open flap. "Is it too much to ask for you to watch him as your own son?" He dipped his chin, and his eyes beheld her with a hint of sorrow.

A few years ago, she would have given anything to bear Reuben a son. He chose another. Her desire was best left buried deep in her soul.

She cleared the regret from her throat. "In our tent

there are ten arms to hold your son. Only a fool would stay away from all that affection." Her cheeks heated. If only he knew how her arms longed to embrace him.

"Toda raba, Mahlah."

Under the moonlight, his eyes sparkled, and for the briefest of seconds, she didn't feel like an awkward neighbor, but like a woman adorned with rubies and gold.

"I will pray for your safety." Her pledge caught in her throat.

His gaze bore down on her like a judge. "And I yours."

Mahlah's brow furrowed. "I am staying in camp."

"You are." He flashed a rugged grin. "With my son, my sister, and four sisters of your own. War doesn't seem so troublesome."

She managed a slight laugh. Did he notice her trembling lips?

Footsteps slapped the ground. Two men strode past. Reuben stepped backward and hesitated.

"Shalom, my mighty Mahlah."

"Shalom." She watched him withdraw to his dwelling.

Before disappearing behind a drape of ramskin, he turned and fixed his gaze upon her. The intensity of his expression made her breath hitch. Was that interest in his eyes, or were the shadows playing tricks on her? More likely, it was gratitude, or worse, pity.

Head down, he entered his tent.

An ache spread across every rib and settled in her side. Would tonight be the last time she laid eyes on Reuben? If it were, she would remember this night as the third worst night of her life.

# 9

The tribes of Israel felled King Sihon and his army in haste. God had given His people victory over the Amorites, but more importantly, God had given the tribes land and cities to inhabit.

After Sihon was defeated, the soldiers of Israel met Og, King of Bashan, in battle. God bestowed another victory on His people, and He bestowed more land.

Her Reuben had not yet returned.

Mahlah and her sisters settled in Moab. The tribes of Israel staked their tents near Shittim.

She remained true to her vow to Reuben and his son. She cared for Jonah while keeping her own sisters out of trouble.

Their elder, Nemuel, rarely spoke to her about tribal business. Her knowledge of clan matters had died with her father in the desert.

As the sun set, she clapped her hands and urged Jonah to catch quail. The boy ran in a circle charging the docile birds and herding them closer to the tents and away from the outskirts of camp. The waft of roasting meat from her kinsmen's fires made her jaw pull tight.

"Hoglah only needs one more hen." She feared Jonah may play this game for hours.

"Come here." Jonah grasped a small bird. When it

stilled, his eyes grew as big as walnuts.

"It's not going."

She bent low, took the quail from him, and slipped it carefully into a sack. "They know they are our food."

He cocked his head. "How they know?"

Had she ever given God's provision much thought? "Well." Her mind filled with Moses' teachings. "God sends us the quail every night. Those we don't catch, go back to be with Him. He will send them again tomorrow."

"Same birds?" Jonah jogged toward a feathered straggler.

"Ah, maybe." Where was an elder to answer such a question?

Jonah stopped pursuing the quail. He craned his neck toward the darkening sky. "Where God live?" He turned and beheld her as if the answer were simple.

The birds in her sack squirmed.

Her face flushed though the evening trade wind lifted her veil. "God is in the cloud over the Tabernacle. He is the pillar of fire that guides us when we travel at night. You have seen Him."

She had beheld these manifestations for seventeen years, but she had also felt God's presence. He'd been in the alcove when she faced the thief. He'd comforted her when her mother died. Even when her father would not gaze at Moses and the snake, she had not been alone. How did she explain these feelings to Jonah?

"God is with our men in battle. He is with your father now." She tousled Jonah's soft, black curls. "God is with us, too, sending us food."

Deep in thought, Jonah's brow furrowed. He touched her bird-filled sack. "Birds go to God."

She snorted a laugh. "That is a question for Moses." Dipping into the satchel, she lifted a bird and held it in front of her face. "Where do you go when you are not feeding our bellies?"

The hen cooed a reply.

"It no talk." Jonah giggled and darted toward the neighboring tents of the tribe of Benjamin.

Putting down the bird, she gave chase and grabbed Jonah's hand. "Come, it's getting late, and you have me speaking to quail." She held the sack in front of him. "We better get these to Hoglah or our stomachs will remain empty."

A squeal broke the calm of the evening.

Jonah huddled close, grasping her skirt.

Two women emerged from tents to the south. An older man stumbled after them. He held an uncapped wineskin. Fermented grape juice sloshed on his hand.

She tried to cover Jonah's eyes.

Mahlah recognized the man as an elder from the tribe of Gad. He had been at meetings with her father. She did not recognize the scandalous garments worn by the women. Skin and jewels glistened in the early starlight. Hardly any cloth covered the women's flesh. A string of gold coins dangled from one woman's waist while the other adorned her belly with a large ruby. Tirzah would have plucked that gem for fun. Praise be her sister was not here to witness this wanton behavior.

The gold-coin-wrapped woman strutted closer, her gold-banded arms outstretched. She mumbled something in a foreign tongue and bent down to Jonah's height, displaying most of her breasts.

Mahlah tugged Jonah farther from the woman, putting distance between them and the woman's wine-tainted breath.

The harlot repeated her gibberish.

"You need a man, not a boy," the elder said. He stumbled toward the talkative woman and kissed her cheek. He glanced at Mahlah. "Isn't my Midianite fawn a beauty? She wants to know if the boy is yours."

"He is not my son." A harshness edged Mahlah's voice. "This is the son of Reuben, Nemuel's heir."

The man gawked as if she was the foreigner speaking gibberish. He snapped his fingers summoning the other girl.

"I will tell her." Wrapping an arm around each woman, he swaggered in the direction of the wilderness, his wineskin beating a rhythm against his back.

Why would an elder of Gad keep company with such women? And to where was the elder escorting those pagans? No leader in camp would accept the display of bared breasts and braided hair worn as a crown. Wasn't the elder worried about offending God?

She shivered. Her father had insulted God, and she had seen the devastating consequences. Every day she and her sisters lived with the hardship from that decision.

"I hungry." Jonah tugged on her robe.

"Yes, we should return home." She peeked at her quail huddled in the sack. They acted asleep, but not Jonah. He watched her, eyes round and awake.

"That woman thought you handsome. You remind me of your father when he played among the tents."

"Yes." Jonah smiled and then darted ahead.

Mahlah quickened her pace. She did not want to think about those half-naked women. The Promised Land from God could not be conquered too soon.

She trudged past the tents of Gad and Benjamin toward the tents of Manasseh. Smoke hung in the air as her clansmen huddled around fires either eating or preparing their roasted quail.

As she approached her tent, only Tirzah and Milcah sat in the cooking courtyard. A small fire blazed between them. Milcah formed patties of ground manna and oil. Jonah discovered the mortar and pestle and pounded air.

"Where's Hoglah?" Mahlah's stomach gurgled after breathing in the aroma of charred meat.

Tirzah placed a stone slab over the fire. She shrugged. "I don't know where she went."

How had her mother and father overseen five children? Mahlah rubbed her pulsing temples.

"Who wants to prepare the quail?"

Tirzah and Milcah exchanged glances, but neither moved to retrieve the sack of birds.

Milcah placed a manna cake on the stone.

"Shall we eat bread then?" Mahlah said. "It's almost ready for our mouths."

Opening the sack, Mahlah let the quail go free. The hens waddled away from the fire.

Jonah jumped around the small clearing, flapping his arms as if he were a bird.

"They go to God." Jonah darted after the quail.

She lunged and grabbed his hand.

"We need to find Hoglah."

He wrinkled his nose and pouted.

Why did she sense that somewhere Hoglah was making a similar face?

# 10

Lifting Jonah to her hip, Mahlah traipsed toward Nemuel's tent. Jonah's head and chest draped over her like a shawl.

The tent tops of Manasseh rose toward a brilliant moon. The glow from the sky illuminated her path. Her sisters were usually home by this hour and resting in the courtyard. Was Hoglah hiding from her? They had not shared harsh words today. Or was her sister grieving? Hoglah had not shed many tears over their father's death.

"I tired."

Mahlah rested her cheek on Jonah's head. "You have traveled all over this camp without complaint. Your grandmother will be proud."

Jonah nodded, barely. His hair tickled her face.

Susanna, Nemuel's wife, huddled next to a low burning fire. She removed roasted quail from a spit. The charred, crisp skin of the fowl caused Mahlah's mouth to fill with saliva. If only Hoglah had seen to her duties, Mahlah's stomach would have been filled with warm meat instead of warm air.

"Jonah is ready for a night's rest." Mahlah jiggled her companion's body. Jonah's eyes opened. He glanced around as if he had woken from a dream in a distant land. She sat near Susanna with Jonah nestled in her lap and dipped her hand in a cleansing jar. "Eat some quail so your stomach does not feel abandoned. Then you will slumber until dawn."

Susanna scraped the last of the meat into a bowl.

Mahlah chose a piece of roasted quail for Jonah.

"Toda raba, Mahlah." Susanna stroked Jonah's hair, smoothing it behind his ear. "I cannot run after my grandson. God spared me from being a cripple after Basemath's birth, but my legs are slower than his."

"Even at my age, Jonah has me lumbering like an ox." She offered Jonah more meat instead of asking after Basemath.

"He will be a great defender of Manasseh." Susanna washed her hands. "No one will be able to catch him."

"Like his father." Mahlah laughed at the memories of her childhood. If only Reuben were here now to chase his son. "I pray for Reuben's return."

"I do as well." Susanna's brow furrowed. "My son cannot return soon enough. Jonah needs his father. And he needs a mother. One swift of foot." Her kinswoman tilted her head and steadied her gaze on Mahlah before shredding the meat.

Mahlah shifted her weight on the stool. Did Susanna believe Mahlah would make a good mother and wife? If this be true, why hadn't Reuben sought a betrothal? Instead, he'd married another. The two-toned tent standing before her bore witness to the addition for Reuben and his deceased wife. Nemuel bragged among the clan how his larger tent would hold heirs aplenty. Nemuel's line was upheld by one lone grandson. Until Reuben came home.

If he came home.

She shuddered. Reuben had to return. Living without him would be worse than watching his happiness with another woman.

"Are your arms tired?" Susanna reached for Jonah. "I can put him on his mat."

The moment Jonah's body lifted from hers, warmth fled. Emptiness filled her lap. The evening breeze chilled her skin, mocking her.

Susanna limped under the weight of her grandson.

Mahlah rose. "Is Basemath inside? Perhaps she can see to Jonah's needs."

"I do not know where my daughter is." Susanna's voice came out strained but not by the burden of carrying Jonah.

Is that why her friend was outside by the fire? Was Basemath not around to help her mother cook the meal? Poor Susanna had to capture the birds by herself.

Where was Basemath? And where was Hoglah? Two girls of the same age. Two girls. Two troublesome girls. Two almost-women.

*Two women.*

Mahlah's heart pulsed a warning. Not like those foreign women? They enticed a leader of Gad to leave camp. Her sister and Basemath wouldn't have followed Moabite men. May it never be.

But would Hoglah and Basemath follow bejeweled girls? Would they drink their wine?

*Oh Lord, when will we be settled in our own land?*

"I will make a search for your daughter." Mahlah held open the tent flap for Susanna and forced a reassuring smile. "Basemath is not fond of me. If I start ordering her around, she will hurry home."

Susanna's eyes glistened. "Bless you, Mahlah. I do

not know when my husband will be home from the assembly."

Hopefully, not soon.

Leaving the tent, Mahlah sprinted toward the Tabernacle. Would Basemath have gone to find her father? Mahlah stood on a crate near the embroidered linen wall and scanned the men gathered to seek their leader, Moses. No young women gathered near the meeting place. She inquired of a few women cooking near the tents of Benjamin. No one had seen two girls unchaperoned. Of course not. Women stared at Mahlah as if she were mad traipsing around in the darkness.

She headed home with fears invading her thoughts. Thankfully, Nemuel occupied himself with his tribal duties and had not ventured home to find his daughter and Hoglah missing.

"Oh Lord, watch over my sister and Basemath. Wherever their foolishness may have taken them."

At least Tirzah and Milcah were perched around a dying fire eating cakes of crushed manna and oil.

Mahlah snatched a flattened cake. "Finish your meal and then go inside the tent."

Tirzah crinkled her nose. "Are you going out again in the dark?"

"Only to find Hoglah." Mahlah popped another morsel of bread into her mouth. "I believe our sister might be with Basemath. She, too, has not made it home, and Susanna is worried."

"You will need light." Milcah stood and brushed off her robe. "I will fetch a lamp, but before I do, we must pray." Milcah's gaze bore into Mahlah's. "Thieves abound in this place."

How could Mahlah have forgotten to pray? God

had provided the quail this night. He had led their soldiers into battle. He was protecting Reuben. And he would protect Hoglah.

She urged her sisters closer and clasped their hands. "Yes, we must pray. How foolish of me to forget." Mahlah bowed her head. "Hear O' Israel, the Lord is our God, the Lord alone."

Tirzah chimed in loudly. "Love the Lord your God with all your heart."

"With all your soul," Milcah continued. "With all your might."

When Milcah finished praying, she squeezed Mahlah's hand.

"Direct my steps, Lord. May Hoglah and Basemath be home soon." Mahlah unclasped her sisters' hands. As she opened her eyes, the right one began to twitch. Why now? She needed keen sight in the dark.

"I will see to the lamp." Milcah hurried into the tent.

"Tirzah, I will need your best sling stones." Mahlah swiped a tear from her cheek and bit her lip. Her sister cherished her collection.

"The whole pouch?"

Mahlah nodded.

"Will I get them back?"

"Not if I use them," Mahlah said.

*Not if they're embedded in a foreigner's face.*

# 11

Holding her lamp high and glancing down every alley, Mahlah raced toward the outlying tents of the tribe of Gad. North would take her to the tribes of Ephraim and Naphtali, and in the direction of the River Jordan. She doubted Hoglah would travel such a distance.

Where were those gold-banded, brazen women escorting the leader of Gad? Had Hoglah and Basemath followed elders from camp? Or worse, had they followed half-naked foreign men to nearby towns? She shuddered at such folly.

Mahlah reached the edge of camp and waited. For what she did not know. A vast desert wilderness stretched before her. Shadowed acacia trees resembled crippled hands ready to pinch her from her home. Was she a fool to venture from her clan, her people? Was Hoglah crying to Noah about her woes? Mahlah blew the tepid air from her lungs. Noah wouldn't listen to one word of complaint from Hoglah. Noah would chase her home and whack a shepherd's staff at her heels. And Basemath? Their neighbor would not have the spine to show her face near Noah's whip.

If Mahlah did not find her sister soon, more shame would be heaped upon the house of Zelophehad. Women who did not sleep under a family tent at night could be exposed as prostitutes.

"Give me wisdom, Adonai."

A donkey brayed off to her left.

Her heart leapt into her throat.

She turned toward the snort.

Holding his hands high, the rider urged the donkey forward with a slight kick.

"Jeremiah?" Her muscles relaxed. A bit. What was he doing on the edge of camp? Why wasn't he with Noah and the livestock?

Mahlah approached Jeremiah's mount. Her clansman cocked his head. Was this his way of questioning her? Noah conversed easily with the mute, but Mahlah scrambled for a manner to explain her situation.

She pointed to her eye. "I'm looking for Hoglah." Splaying five fingers, she grasped her thumb and held it to her breast. "Me." She grasped the pointing finger. "Noah."

Jeremiah grinned at the mention of her sister's name. Perhaps her sister had jabbed him a few times with the same finger.

Rubbing her middle finger, she said, "Hoglah." With a sweeping motion, she indicated the wilderness.

"I saw." She touched her eye again. "A leader." Straightening, she puffed out her chest. "Go with two women." She displayed two fingers and pulled some hair free from its covering. Honestly, how did Noah manage with this young man?

Nodding, Jeremiah held up four fingers and pinched the smallest finger.

Youngest brother?

He grabbed his next finger and pointed into the outskirts.

Eli, Jeremiah's brother, was missing, too.

"Take me with you." She patted her shoulder and stroked the donkey's mane.

Eyes wide, Jeremiah shook his head.

Mahlah wedged a fist against her hip and glared at the shepherd. Hopefully he could see her determination in her lamplight. "I'm going." She took a step. Another stomp. Three.

Jeremiah jumped from the donkey. He caught her and laced his hands mimicking an assist to mount.

She didn't need help getting on a mount. She shook her head and handed him her lamp.

Praise be. God had provided an escort. A clansman to protect her well-being and her reputation. She slung her shoulders back and mounted the donkey. "Toda raba, God of Jacob."

Her mute shepherd grinned.

"And Jeremiah."

He pointed to himself and then returned the lamp.

"Do you know where to go?" She shrugged and placed a hand to shield her eyes as if she were looking for something.

Jeremiah wedged the reins under his armpit and steepled his hands over and over.

"You know where a town is?"

Nodding, he turned the donkey into the night.

After a fair amount of riding, a glow banished the darkness. The aroma of burning wood hung over the landscape. Campfires. Jeremiah quickened his pace.

They trod closer to the outskirts of a Moabite town. Orange and amber flames brightened the indentation of a huge livestock pit. The ground rose into a mound on the far side of the sunken arena. Fire raged from an altar on top of the hill. Sparks spewed toward the stars.

Mahlah dismounted and rushed closer to the pit. Even with the warm waft of air from the raging fire, she shivered. Her skin tingled as if the embers singed her skin. This spectacle was not a feast, nor a celebration, for a cast image emerged from the vibrant flames.

Dancers flung their bodies round and round in front of a statue of a man whose head was longer than a flute. With no heed of decency, women pranced in a circle naked. Only the dancers' gold armlets and anklets covered flesh. Pagans wiggled their hips in a disgusting manner. Saliva seeped into Mahlah's mouth bringing with it the taste of olive oil from Tirzah's cake. Her stomach flipped like a newly netted fish.

"Lord, help us."

To his credit, Jeremiah did not ogle the spectacle before their eyes. His gaze scanned the mass of people whose bodies writhed in the dirt like worms. Mounds of discarded clothing cluttered the pit. Guttural moaning rose from the shadowed ground.

Mahlah heard Moses' voice reciting the Commandments of God. *You shall have no other gods.* Definitely not this oblong-headed idol.

Her sister knew God's commands. What possessed her to come to this pit?

Someone tapped her shoulder.

She gasped as a surge of frigid water shot through her body.

Jeremiah.

Her heart settled into place.

He pointed to a small huddle of people.

His brother Eli, Hoglah, and Basemath swayed in a circle, their arms slung around each other's shoulders. Praise be their bodies were fully clothed. Her bow-strung nerves eased a notch, but only one, for she had to be on guard entering a pagan orgy.

Leaving her lamp near the donkey, she followed Jeremiah into the mass of revelers. With his broad shoulders and logs for arms, Jeremiah shoved frenzied Hebrews and heathens out of his path. Ignorant, drunken grins welcomed his aggression as a friendly embrace.

Mahlah ripped her sister from Eli's hold.

"We need to leave." She barked the command like her father and then wrapped an arm around her sister's waist for support.

Hoglah's head bobbed, but no recollection dawned in her half-lidded eyes. Her body was a baking stone upon Mahlah's hip.

Basemath twirled, arms outstretched, as if to join another grouping.

Mahlah gripped her arm and tugged the girl toward her. "We are going back to camp."

For once, Basemath was speechless. She focused on Mahlah's headband as if it were bejeweled and not a band of leather.

Eli thrashed at his brother's hold. Jeremiah bent Eli's arm and held it behind his brother's back. Eli swore. Jeremiah used his brother as a battering ram to escape the pit.

"Come. This way." Mahlah's shrieks disturbed a kissing couple. The man muttered at her in her own language. Had he no shame?

Why were her people participating in this idol worship? Did Moses know of this debauchery? Is that why Moses called a meeting of the tribal elders?

Head down and with muscles flaming, Mahlah

did her best to propel Hoglah and Basemath in Jeremiah's wide wake.

"Use your feet." She made sure her words echoed in the girl's ears.

Basemath sputtered a laugh.

The stench of fermented grapes filled Mahlah's nostrils. Basemath stank the same as that scantily-clad harlot in camp.

Swinging her arms as if trying to crawl after their clansmen, Basemath's golden armlets glistened in the firelight. She wore more trinkets than the altar prostitutes.

Hoglah's head dropped like a boulder upon Mahlah's shoulder.

"Lord, give me strength. I am but a yoke between two oxen." Using her strong leg muscles, Mahlah pushed against the ground and barreled forward.

A cloaked form blocked her path.

She was in no mood for a confrontation with a drunken, love-struck Moabite or a bare-breasted Midianite.

Glancing upward, she stilled.

"Ah, we meet again, lioness," the familiar voice hissed. "You have come to save your cubs."

# 12

Mahlah recognized that robe with its crimson and purple collar, and the black forms spotting the drape of linen. Why did she have to lay eyes on this bandit once more? Milcah's observation echoed in her brain. *He had blood on his feet.*

"You stole our goat." Her proclamation carried over the moaning of the revelers. Perhaps if she kept her voice strong, he would not notice the gentle shake of her legs.

Cackling, the bandit clapped his hands.

Was he mocking her?

"Look around, lioness. Why would I have need of a goat when there are better things to sacrifice?" The liar's glare fell on an unsteady Hoglah.

Mahlah's belly hollowed. She had heard of babies being thrown into the fire as offerings to pagan gods. Certainly not women? Not tonight. Not her sister. Not a daughter of Zelophehad. If only her sister and Basemath weren't pinning her blade and sling stones against her body.

Hoglah bent forward, a hand clasped to her mouth.

"We must get you home." She stared into the dark, squinting eyes of the thief. "Aren't you going to let us pass? My sister is ill."

The man could have been a statue, for not a wrinkle of compassion flickered in his fang-toothed mask of a face.

He nodded toward the altar, not one piece of hair shifting from his greased mane. "I believe these women were on their way to dance."

"May it never be!" A rapid thudding echoed in her ears. "Our God forbids celebrations before an idol."

"Such a shame." He pouted. "You do not let your cubs romp and play."

"Not with a thief who tortures a nursing goat." The truth stormed from her lips, but no ally stirred to notice. Would not a single Hebrew come to her defense?

"I am not a thief." His rebuke reverberated through her chest and sobered her blissful sister.

His charcoal-lined eyes widened and then became slits as if he were trying to mesmerize her with his being.

A tiny twitch fluttered her right eyelid. Not now. She couldn't afford her eye to droop and water. Strength would get her home, not tears. Not in this soulless place.

She blinked. *Lord, bless your servant.*

"The truth does not change." She rolled her shoulders back, dislodging her kin a step and bolstering her height. Thank goodness her eyelid stayed open. "You took our goat to sacrifice."

He laughed. His high-pitched, humiliating squeal engaged a few half-dressed women and the men feasting on their nakedness.

"What have I stolen from you?" He flung his arms as if addressing a court of judges. "One swollen goat." He pointed his finger at a nearby man. "Only one." He puffed his chest like a pharaoh's pillow. "Your people are taking this land city by city. You spill the blood of Amorites and sup in their stone houses."

Muttering grew among the worshipers closest to the thief. Hissing like snakes, the heathens beheld her with contempt.

"Our God gave us this land." Would her challenge rally some of her people to cast away their passions and voice their faith? Someone? Anyone?

"Which god would that be? Hmmm? For I know them all. I have prayed to them all." His taunts grew louder. "I have slit open bellies to them all. Offered hearts and organs to them all."

"You. Do. Not. Know. My God." Mahlah's teeth clenched. How dare this pagan ridicule the God of Abraham and compare Him with images of stone and clay.

A lark *swooshed* from a tree over her head. The flap of its wings rallied her heartbeat even more. *Lord, I need Your shalom.*

"Balaam, enough of these harsh words. Start the sacrifices." A long-haired girl sashayed toward the bandit and slipped an arm under his ruby-studded cloak. Her armlets and rings glistened with almost as many jewels as the thief's.

At least Mahlah had a name to curse: Balaam. But now she knew her foe held the position of a pagan priest. Her temples ached.

Balaam stepped closer, jerking the woman forward. "Have you spoken to your god, lioness. I have seen his heavenly warriors and I, Balaam son of Beor, am alive and able to speak of it."

The beauty at Balaam's side dropped to her knees and kissed his fingers.

Mahlah ignored the spectacle of the woman groveling at the priest's feet and held his serpent-eyed gaze. "If you have seen and spoken to my God, then you know He is a living God."

Basemath struggled against Mahlah's hold. "The ground is moving."

"I must get my sisters home." She pushed the girls around Balaam.

"To your tent?" Balaam snorted. "My, what comforts your God provides. The worshipers of Baal live in a city of brick and stone. Are you sure you do not want to celebrate with us?"

Thrusting his hips toward her, Balaam gyrated, pleasing his dancer. Mahlah gagged on the bile pooling in her throat.

Would this nightmare never end? How dare this fool show contempt for her and her God? Was this a test of her faith? A test for the house of Zelophehad? Her father had grumbled against God's provision. May it never be said that she uttered a whine. She would not allow this filth of a man to trample upon the name of her God.

She released the hands of Basemath and Hoglah and urged them to make their way farther from Balaam's blockade.

"Your worship is not our worship. We worship the One True God. The God of Abraham, Isaac, and Jacob."

Balaam spit in the dirt. "All murderers and thieves."

*Whap.* She slapped him. Firm and hard and without a simple thought.

In a blur, he cinched her wrist with his long-fingered hand.

Her palm throbbed as he held her fast. Was this

the same helplessness her goat had felt?

Gritting her teeth, she glared at him as fierce and wild as the lion he claimed her to be. Her body shook, not from fear, but from the overwhelming disgust and fury she hurled at this man. She dropped her weight, finding an inner balance. This priest held no power over her or her God, and she would resist the slightest tug to keep her dignity in this immoral pit.

Commotion. The clop of hooves. Squealing. Braying. All came from the direction Jeremiah had traveled.

The dancing woman screamed.

Balaam released Mahlah's wrist and leapt to the side.

Eli clung to a bucking donkey, its teeth snapping at anyone or anything that came close.

Mahlah dove away from Balaam.

"It's gone mad," Eli screamed. "Help me."

Her clansman had sobered fast.

Couples scrambled from the crazy beast.

The pagan woman clung to Balaam, her gold armlets a beacon against the black animal forms on his cloak.

"Haven't Midianites seen asses?" Balaam jerked and attempted to free himself from the frightened dancer.

Mahlah ran, grabbed Hoglah and Basemath, and did a fast waddle down the path the donkey had cleared.

Jeremiah waved them onward toward the outskirts of the pit.

"Flee to your sheep skin city," Balaam shouted.

She swatted away his jeer like a pesky fly and raced into the dark.

How were they going to get their donkey back? And Eli?

Placing two fingers into his mouth, Jeremiah whistled.

Hoglah and Basemath covered their ears, complaining.

She welcomed the shrill ring.

At a full-on trot, their donkey sprinted out of the pit. Jeremiah ushered them after his donkey and frenzied brother.

*Toda raba, Adonai.*

Several paces from the pit, Mahlah slowed her steps and caught her breath. Her arm muscles burned from carrying the weight of her sister and neighbor. The feel of Balaam's grip still lingered on her wrist. She breathed deep and filled her lungs with smoke-tainted air. To her, the breeze was as fresh as the breeze on a manna-picking morning. The pit didn't hold her, and most importantly, it didn't hold her sister. She couldn't bear to lose another family member.

She and Jeremiah helped Basemath mount the calmed donkey. Eli, mostly sober, didn't protest his loss of a ride.

"I'll walk," Hoglah said. She stared past Mahlah into the silhouettes of a grove of acacia trees.

Hearing her sister speak without a slur made Mahlah walk as tall as the night-covered branches. Should she demand an answer to her sister's foolishness? Later, when they were alone.

"You may hold our lamp." Mahlah retrieved their light and handed it to her sister.

A low drum beat echoed in the distance. Visions of the fiery altar sent a chill over Mahlah's flesh. Praise God they had been delivered from that pagan priest.

Her mind wandered to their camp. Were her sisters asleep or huddled in their tent waiting for her return? In Jeremiah's absence, and with double the flocks to care for, Noah would not have made it into camp to check on the young ones. Mahlah only hoped that Moses had much to discuss with the tribal leaders and that Nemuel was delayed at the Tent of Meeting, for what explanation could she give to him about the absence and state of his daughter? Would he blame her leadership? Or worse, Hoglah? The daughters of Zelophehad did not need another tongue lashing.

*Oh Lord, give me wisdom and save me from another pit.*

Her eye twitched and began to water.

# 13

Mahlah became light of foot as she came within a few strides of the tents of the tribes of Israel. How beautiful was the rise and fall of animal skins over the landscape. A home did not need brick or rock for its foundation.

She waved at Jeremiah.

"I," she pointed to herself, "will take Basemath and Hoglah." She indicated the other two women. "Home." Cresting her fingers, she made a tent with her hands.

Eli rubbed his head. "Why blather to him? Take your sister and go."

Mahlah glowered at the pit reveler. "Jeremiah escorted me into the wilderness. Not you."

"Dull your tongue," Eli snapped. "No one needs to be the wiser. Surely, you agree." He nodded toward Basemath draped over the donkey. "She needs a drink of water or a dousing."

"You should know." Mahlah brushed by Eli and gently shook her neighbor. "Wake up. We must get you home."

Basemath sat and grimaced. "My body hurts."

"It will feel better in the morn." Hoglah came alongside Mahlah. "Let us help you dismount."

Sliding from the donkey, Basemath's gold armlets

glistened against the dark-brown fur of her mount. The animal sidestepped showing more life than the idol worshiped in the pit.

Each taking a shoulder, Mahlah and Hoglah ushered Basemath toward her tent.

Jeremiah stalked forward. He pointed to his lips and then to his palm at the base of his middle finger.

"No tell Noah," Mahlah said. "Definitely not." She craned her neck and gave Eli a raised-eyebrow challenge. "I am the eldest of our family. I will decide who we tell and when."

"I am not the eldest," Eli said, making sure Jeremiah could see his lips. "We won't speak of this."

"I don't feel well," Basemath moaned.

Eli leapt onto the donkey. "Get her to bed." He kicked his mount. "Shalom."

Jeremiah jogged after his brother toward their flocks.

"If Nemuel is awake, there will be no peace." She made her way to the broadest path through the tents of Manasseh.

Sure-footed and glimpsing every shadow, Hoglah kept one stride ahead of Mahlah.

"What will we tell Nemuel and Susanna? Nemuel's wrath will be worse than father's."

"Hah. Not by much." Shouldn't her sister have thought of the consequences before wandering into the wilderness with Basemath? Mahlah adjusted her cousin's weight. "I spoke with Susanna when I brought Jonah home. Nemuel was meeting with the tribal leaders and Moses. Let us hope every leader wishes to be heard tonight."

"Oh, my ears." Basemath opened her eyes, blinked, and then slammed them shut.

As they neared their droopy-sided tent, Mahlah slowed. "I will carry on with Basemath."

Hoglah shook her head. "I cannot go inside our tent. Let me stay with Susanna."

Mahlah's mind spun. Was her sister still upset about the men of Asher being sent away? What was troubling her to make her run off with Basemath? Clenching her teeth, Mahlah stifled a rebuke. An argument would only bring curious neighbors to their tent flap. Their family's reputation did not need to be whispered about among the water jars. She breathed out and flexed her aching knuckles.

"You have to come home."

"I will. In the morning."

Did her sister think taking charge of this family was easy?

"What is one night?" Mahlah's tone sharpened.

A low whine rumbled from Basemath's lips.

"I don't want Milcah or Tirzah to see me," Hoglah whispered. "Or smell me. I will come home washed with a belly full of manna."

Hoglah was correct. They would never fool Milcah if she was awake. How would they explain the odor of wine and fragrant smoke?

"We cannot lie to our sisters." Mahlah changed direction. "Maybe it's best if you sleep in Nemuel's tent."

Hoglah's brow furrowed. "You agree?"

"It seems we finally do on something."

Mahlah eased Basemath's weight onto Hoglah and then poked her head inside Nemuel's tent. Praise God, her uncle was nowhere in sight. She motioned for Susanna to come outside.

Susanna rose from her mat beside Jonah, picked

up a lamp, and followed Mahlah out of the tent.

"What has happened to my daughter?" Susanna stroked Basemath's cheek.

"I'm tired and my stomach aches." Basemath's words were one long moan.

"She needs water and rest." Mahlah and Hoglah exchanged glances. "Hoglah can stay with you tonight. She will fetch water and help if Jonah wakes."

Susanna skimmed a hand over Basemath's jeweled armlets. "Why is she dressed like this? Where did you find her?"

Mahlah would not bear false witness. Especially not to an elder's wife and close relative.

"I found her outside of the camp near Shittim."

The ashen half-circles under Susanna's eyes deepened. She pressed a hand to her lips.

"Perhaps it is best if we talk in the morning." Mahlah motioned for Hoglah to get Basemath to bed.

Hoglah handed her the lamp and helped the girl inside the tent.

"Our elders need to hear what is happening not far from our camp." Mahlah withheld further explanation.

Susanna nodded. Her eyes glistened with tears in the light of the lamp. "I wouldn't know what to tell my husband. Why would our daughter wander off?"

Mahlah wondered the same thing. In the morning, she expected to get answers from both girls. But they were not the only ones who needed to confess their actions. Eli shared in the blame.

"It may only be a small comfort, but I saw leaders of our people joining in the festivities."

"God forgive us," Susanna rasped. "What would I have done if you had not searched for her?" She kissed

Mahlah's cheek. "Bless you."

Susanna shuffled inside the tent.

Ducking under the guy-line, Mahlah rounded the corner and returned home. Alone. Her conscience nagged her. Would her mother have let Hoglah sleep in Nemuel's tent? Or would she have brought the night's grievances to Nemuel in haste?

Mahlah grabbed hold of her tent flap and tugged it open. Her sisters had not tied it shut.

Inside, Tirzah and Milcah lay on their mats. The glow of a lamp revealed piles of stones cluttering the ground near Tirzah. If sorting rocks kept her sisters out of heathen worship pits, she would have the whole family partake. Being a mother and father to four girls was exhausting. Again, she wondered how her mother had managed five daughters.

Tirzah stirred and sat. "Where's Hoglah? Did you find her?"

"Yes, but she is spending the night with Susanna." Mahlah made it seem commonplace. She unfurled her mat and placed it near her sisters. "Hoglah will be home tomorrow."

"Does she need to help with Jonah?" Milcah mumbled the question still curled on her side.

"No, but it's time to rest."

Mahlah's body sank into the thick woven reeds of her mat. Her bones had walked half of the night and chased Jonah half of the day. Her mouth lacked the will to mutter a prayer for Reuben's safe return. She would pray twofold tomorrow and prepare an offering for her family.

She was awakened from a refreshing sleep by a man's wailing.

Was it real or a dream about the pit, or—? She

sprang upright and instinctively searched the tent for snakes. Nothing moved. No light of dawn crept through the seams. Night lingered.

Mahlah licked her parched lips and listened.

The piteous wailing echoed nearby. It sounded like—

*Oh no, no, no.* She leapt to her feet, pulse hammering in her temples. Nemuel was shrieking.

"What's wrong?" Milcah sat and grabbed her knees.

"Stay here." Mahlah tore at the tent ties. "Do not leave our home." Her tone sharpened. "Something's not right."

She raced from the flap.

Nemuel stood hunched in the middle of the wide path.

A few neighboring clansmen emerged from their tents.

Their leader wept, tearing at his hair.

"A plague rages in my tent."

# 14

How could this be? Mahlah had left Nemuel's tent only hours before. Hoglah and Susanna weren't feverish. Basemath had been sleepy from drinking wine, but what Mahlah saw of her skin, it wasn't pocked with sores. Mahlah could hardly think through her uncle's screams. Was God judging Hoglah's and Basemath's time in the pit? Was this sickness a result of their disobedience? But why the whole tent? She and her sisters lived, even though her father had challenged God and Moses' leadership? She had been in the pit with her sister and Basemath and no plague ailed her flesh?

Her chest tightened as she bent low before her elder. "Are they alive?" She fisted her hands and readied for his answer.

Nemuel's head bobbed, but it was not a definite shake.

Mahlah blinked back tears. "I will take care of them." Mahlah stood and jabbed a finger at a nearby couple. "We will need water to bathe their bodies. Lots of water. And lots of jars." She pointed to another clanswoman. "Bring strips of cloth."

"No," Nemuel shouted. He charged at her like a wild boar. "You will not go near my heir. The curse of Zelophehad has entered my tent. Your sister's presence has diseased my family."

Heat surged through Mahlah's limbs. How dare Nemuel accuse her sister of causing this plague? She and her sisters were not cursed. They lived and breathed before God like everyone else. She had to dismiss his accusation before gossip filled the whole camp. Or, God forbid, kinsmen picked up stones to kill her.

"We are not cursed." Mahlah held out her hands and displayed her arms. "Look at me." She addressed the gathering crowd of Manasseh. "My skin does not carry a rash. No boils fester on my arms."

"Or mine."

"Mine, too."

Mahlah turned to see Milcah and Tirzah with arms raised, huddled at the front of the crowd of her clansmen. Her heart swelled with pride at their boldness. Even though they had disobeyed her.

"Do not say we brought a plague." Loud and definite, Mahlah proclaimed her family's innocence right to their leader's forlorn face.

She stepped away. This anger would do neither of them any good. Their loved ones needed care. "You are overcome with grief. I know the depths." Mahlah leaned close. "Your daughter wandered from camp and was out near Shittim. Moses will know if this is a punishment from God. Seek him straight away."

Nemuel's jaw gaped. "Liar!" Arms flailing her direction, he stumbled. "How dare you blame this sickness on my daughter."

Gasps came from the gathering crowd.

Mahlah needed to refute the elder's scorn before her kin doubted her truthfulness and her standing. Nemuel's pride was keeping her from tending the ill before they succumbed to the plague. Did he believe there wasn't any hope of a cure? She needed to get inside the tent, tend to her family, and ask forgiveness. Fast.

"I have witnesses," she proclaimed to her relatives. Truth would be told this night no matter the consequences. Death would not take her sister or Jonah without a fight. "Men from Manasseh will support my words. My family remains faithful to the One True God."

"What men will speak for you?" Spit flew from Nemuel's lips.

"Seek out Eli and Jeremiah. They escorted me tonight." She would not reveal more in such a public place.

Abishua shouldered his way to the front of the crowd. "I just saw my sons in the field. They are not sick with fever."

If Eli did not suffer, why did her sister and Basemath? Surely Eli's actions were offensive to God?

She shuffled away from the leaders, closer to the tent. "I have given you a witness who can speak to my truthfulness. Now let me tend to my sister and my kin. I am not afraid of a fever." Hadn't she given her word to Reuben that she would oversee his son? And what about Susanna? The woman had been so tired this evening and desperate of spirit. A sob threatened to break free from Mahlah's chest. "I beg of you. Pray to God for our family and for our tribe. I cannot bear another loss. Am I not already an orphan?"

Abishua wrapped an arm around Nemuel's shoulders. "Come. Let us pray as Moses has instructed the elders."

Nemuel collapsed into his relative's arms.

Women hurried forward with water jars and strips of cloth.

Praise God some people were listening this night.

"May the Lord bless you." Mahlah accepted their provisions.

Her clanswomen nodded and scattered. Their sandals did not move one step toward Nemuel's dwelling.

"This disease is elsewhere in the camp," a woman said. "Leaders from the tribes of Gad and Simeon have fallen ill. Their wives are hysterical."

Was God judging the tribal leaders for their worship of Baal? Is that why Nemuel was so distraught? Had Moses spoken of God's wrath at the council meeting?

Too many thoughts clouded her mind. She might as well have been caught in a whirlwind. *Adonai, give me wisdom and forgive our transgressions.*

Milcah came up beside her sloshing water on Mahlah's bare feet. Tirzah's arms were full of ripped linen.

"Oh sisters." Mahlah almost wept. "You must let me go in alone. I could not bear if you fell ill. Stay outside and pray for our people."

Her sisters did not utter agreement. They scowled as if she had spoken foreign babble.

"We can help." Milcah adjusted her load.

"Yes, you can. When I need water or more bandages, you can set them at the tent flap." Mahlah furled her brow and scowled, but her harsh expression faltered. "Please, sisters. Wait here with our people. Show God your faithfulness and listen to me."

"Fine." Milcah lowered her jar. "But if the tent gets too quiet, we will rush inside."

"I wouldn't expect less." A tear dribbled down Mahlah's cheek. "Our God will protect me from the plague. I was with our family all day." *And night.* "I am strong." She hefted the water jar.

Tirzah stuffed strips of linen in Mahlah's belt.

After kissing the tops of her sisters' heads, Mahlah dipped inside Nemuel's tent, dreading what she would find inside. She mumbled a prayer.

The vast ramskin walls stitched to add room for Reuben and his wife, now reminded her of a large tomb. Bodies lay on mats, unmoving. A groan welcomed her entrance. She had no hand to cover her nose and shelter her from the odor of sweat and raw flesh. Fighting a gag from the smell, she sucked in a breath through her mouth.

Jonah lay next to Susanna. Mahlah rushed to the boy and knelt beside him. She raised his head slowly and supported it while she dipped a cup in the water jar. His hair raged hot against her arm.

"Drink, little one."

"I hurt." Jonah's eyes did not open to greet her, but he sipped the water.

"I am right here, but you must drink. It will cool the fever."

She fumbled to moisten a cloth and place it on his brow. "The Lord bless you, Jonah."

The boy's eyes fluttered open. Even overcome with fever and ache, they reminded her of his father's eyes, unnervingly beautiful with bronze specks illuminating the deep brown.

Jonah's lips curved slightly, but a smile did not come forth.

Susanna struggled to shift onto her side. Her droopy-lidded gaze fell on her grandchild.

"Save my babies. I have lived my life."

Mahlah's throat grew tight. "God will save all of you. He will answer our petitions. Many are praying for your healing." Mahlah placed a wet cloth on her friend's forehead. The woman radiated heat like a blazing fire. She tugged on Susanna's neckline and laid another cloth on her chest. Handing her a cup, Mahlah encouraged her to drink.

Hoglah called out for water.

Lunging toward her sister, Mahlah did not care if she splashed water all over the tent.

"Oh, sister." Mahlah offered Hoglah a cup. "Tell me. When did you become ill? I did not see any signs when I left you."

Hoglah shimmied to sit. Her forehead wrinkled. "I don't remember. I went to sleep next to Basemath and woke up in pain. I thought I was dreaming, but now it hurts to see."

At the mention of her name, Basemath coughed. She panted like a donkey run hard in the heat.

Mahlah set a rag on the girl's head. Black charcoal lines streaked her cousin's cheeks. Mahlah wiped away the mess, hoping she could wipe away the memories of the pit. Why had she sought such a place? Was Eli to blame? She shook the questions from her mind. Once everyone was healed, she would seek the answers.

Basemath swiped a hand over her forehead, knocking off the wet linen. Her gold armlets glistened, catching the lamplight. Golden embers brightened and faded as if taunting Mahlah.

From one to another to another, Mahlah forced her loved ones to sip water. Where was the healing? Tears welled in her eyes, but she did not let them fall. She did not have time to tend to them.

"God of Jacob," she called out. "Heal my family. Don't take my sister or Jonah from me. Didn't I promise Reuben that I would care for his son? I vowed to my mother that I would care for her daughters. I cannot bear anymore heartache. Forgive any wrongdoing."

Jonah whimpered.

Standing in the center of the tent, Mahlah raised her arms toward the ceiling. "God, please. You have spared our whole camp from our enemies. What is saving four lives? Honor my request, O Lord." Her lips quivered. "When have I not served you? Even tonight, you provided an escort for me. You led us to the pit and home again. Is this the end you desire?"

Crying, Jonah curled into himself.

She picked up the boy, his skin baking from the inside out.

"Oh, God." Her plea rumbled from her throat as she rocked Jonah to quiet his sobs.

Basemath rolled on her side. Her hand touched her forehead again, dislodging the cool cloth.

Even in illness, that girl antagonized Mahlah.

A design on a gold armlet illuminated in the light. A shape like that of a long head. Was that a divot for an eye?

She shivered at the remembrance of the statue of Baal. The vile dancing. Balaam's sneer. *Curse you, pagans!* Images of false gods did not belong in the Israelite camp.

Setting Jonah down as gently and possible, she stormed toward Basemath like the lioness that heathen priest had claimed her to be.

# 15

*You shall have no other gods before me.* The command from her God roared through her conscience. Mahlah ripped the gold armlet from her cousin's arm. Had Balaam given her cousin this trinket on purpose? Did the sorcerer delight in branding a Hebrew girl with the image of a pagan god? Or had another bestowed this golden image on Basemath? Even sober, Basemath would have accepted jewelry of value.

Mahlah covered the engraved image with her palm and fled from the tent.

A collective gasp came from the crowd of her kinsmen gathered outside. Did they believe her family dead? Nemuel collapsed into the dirt.

"Stoke the cooking fire." Mahlah grabbed a log and threw it on the waning orange coals. Sparks burst into the night shadows. "Hurry. We don't have much time."

"My wife," Nemuel wailed.

Milcah and Tirzah raced in front of an older woman and poked at the growing flames with sticks. An aunt came forward and arranged new wood on the stirred-up fire.

Mahlah held the armlet with Baal's image over the fire. She dropped the gold band in the center of the fiery coals.

"Char that gold. It belonged to a pagan priest."

Her sisters gasped.

Another clanswoman screamed and scampered from the fire pit.

"What is this madness?" Nemuel rose and stumbled toward the flames. "There are no idols in my tent."

"There aren't now, but I can't be sure your daughter wasn't given any other tainted gold." Mahlah swiped her hands together to remove the feel of the band. "Every jewel in your tent must go into the fire."

"We will burn it all good." Tirzah placed more kindling on the rebirthed flames.

"No, no. It cannot be." Nemuel reached for her sleeve.

Mahlah did not have time to argue with her elder or explain her actions further. Dodging his grasp, she fisted her hand. "Do not challenge me. I know of what I speak." She scanned the crowd for Abishua, but he had abandoned his kinsman. "That was the first trinket to go, and it won't be the last."

"Leader," Milcah said. "Let's ask God for mercy."

Others echoed her sister's request for prayer.

Nemuel nodded; despair etched in his brow.

Mahlah dashed inside the tent and filled a satchel with all of Basemath's jewelry. Not a single bauble remained on the girl's body.

*You shall have no other gods before me.*

Had Basemath given any gold to her mother or Hoglah? Mahlah couldn't risk disobedience to God's command. She slipped every ring, bracelet, or bead into her bag. Her gaze swept the tent for the tiniest of stones. She would not let Balaam and his false gods endanger her family further.

"Curse you, Balaam. Curse you for stealing our goat. Curse you for trying to defile my family."

One step. Two steps. Three. She whipped open the tent flap and hurried toward the fire's roaring flame.

"The Lord is our God, the Lord Alone," she shouted as she tossed gold and jewels into the vibrant yellow-orange blaze. "Do not remove these from the ashes. We will bury them, so the plague does not strike our tribe anew." Turning, she spoke, half to herself, half to the ramskin in front of her, "I must change the face cloths."

"I will assist you." Milcah abandoned her stick.

Tirzah stomped toward the tent. "We want to help Hoglah."

"Wait." Mahlah held out her hand. Her nerves twisted tight. Should she allow her sisters to tend the sick? Was the engraved band the only cause of the plague? She licked her lips, but no moisture clung to her skin.

*God, give me wisdom.*

"You shouldn't worry." Milcah rocked on her sandals as if was contemplating sprinting into the tent. "There is no sign of the plague on your skin."

"What if it comes later?" Mahlah bit her lip. "I don't know what I would do if I caused my family to fall ill."

"We won't get sick," Tirzah offered. "We prayed."

If only these little ones knew the depths of evil she had seen near Shittim.

"I believe in you, Mahlah. Like father did." Milcah stepped closer to the tent flap. "With three of us tending our family, the plague doesn't have a chance."

Mahlah opened the flap. A windstorm would be easier to thwart than her sisters.

"Lord, honor our devotion," she said as she ushered her sisters inside.

In the flickering lamplight, Hoglah sat bent forward, her arms resting on her knees. "I don't feel right. My head is pounding."

Milcah offered her sister a cup. "You're speaking. That's a good sign."

Mahlah checked Jonah's forehead. His skin had cooled from earlier. "Praise be to the God of Abraham, Isaac, and Jacob. The fevers seem to be going."

Jonah grasped her arm. "I hungry."

Mahlah's heart soared to the heavens at Jonah's request. "It's almost time to gather fresh manna."

Tirzah's hand shot toward the tent top. "I'll go gather it."

"So loud." Basemath rolled onto her side. "My ears hurt."

"That's from fermented grapes, not our voices." Susanna struggled to rise from her mat. "I would have said I dreamed being ill, but my body is like one of those rags."

"To see you move is a blessing." Mahlah reached over and squeezed her friend's hand. "Praise the Lord. He has answered our prayers and spared this tent."

A melody came to Mahlah. "Our God is the faithful God. He keeps His covenant of love. To a thousand generations."

"Of those who love Him," Milcah sang.

"And keep His commands." Tirzah's voice rang out strong.

Hoglah joined in the singing.

Basemath covered her ears. "This is causing me more pain."

Jonah giggled. Once. But even a small snort was a

victory.

Mahlah set Jonah on her hip. She offered the boy a drink, her muscles relaxing with every sip he took.

A few women peeked into the tent.

"Manna is forming, one woman said. "We will harvest some for you."

"Toda raba." Mahlah swayed side-to-side with Jonah in her arms. "We have a hungry boy, and we have plenty of fire to heat a stone."

A smile of gratitude graced Susanna's face. "Husband, come sup with us."

Nemuel shuffled inside the tent, tears flooding his face.

"My family lives. God has answered my prayers." He embraced his wife and almost knocked Mahlah over as he wrestled Jonah from her arms.

The elder lifted the boy in the air. "My heir is alive. God has shown us His favor."

*Favor?* Mahlah stood, gaped-mouthed, as Nemuel smothered Jonah with kisses. God had shown mercy, but didn't her kinsman care about what had drawn his daughter into a pagan pit? What about her own faithfulness to family and to their God?

Another woman barged into the tent. Now that the plague was gone, the entrance had become a trade route.

"Noah?"

Fists embedded in her hips, her sister said, "I'm glad there is rejoicing in here because Abishua is raising havoc in my field."

# 16

Mahlah's knees almost buckled as she rushed toward her sister. In all the chaos of the night, she hadn't sent word to Noah about the pit nor the plague. She didn't want to pull their shepherdess from the fields after the accusations that her family relied too heavily on their kin. And with the plague, well, Noah would have barged right into Nemuel's tent and chastised their wayward neighbor, fever or no fever. That possibility could come to fruition even now if Noah lingered.

She grasped Noah's hand and pulled her outside and toward their empty tent. The rest of their family did not need to hear the sordid details from the pit.

Huffing, Noah followed.

"I cannot believe you left the camp without me. Without a word." Noah's harsh tone held a hint of hurt. "I knew I should have questioned Jeremiah's absence." She paced back and forth, her arms berating the air. "Why does one need a donkey after dark?"

Leaning forward, Mahlah grabbed hold of her sister and kissed her cheek.

"Oh, Noah. I needed you here. If I did not return, someone would have to care for Tirzah and Milcah." She inched backward. "How much do you know?"

"Everything." Noah's deep brown eyes bore into

95

Mahlah. "Our elder was furious. He demanded to know if his sons worshiped Baal. He said you named them as witnesses to your journey and the lawlessness at the pagan orgy." Noah rubbed her forehead. "I should have known to question Jeremiah when he returned with Eli. That man has never spent one night with his father's livestock in all our years together."

"Where is Eli now?" Abishua had a quick temper.

"Taking care of our sheep."

"What?" Flashes of the reprimands on the trail caused her stomach to cramp. She readied a rebuke. "I don't want—"

"Abishua insisted." Noah poured a drink from the lone water jar alongside their tent. "I knew you'd be upset, but he wanted me to come and help you tend to our kin. This is fitting for Eli. Jeremiah was so distraught by what he saw in the pit that only I could understand his motions and relay his words to his father."

Mahlah, too, wished to banish Balaam's face and his followers from her memory. "Until tonight, I never realized how frustrating it is to speak with Jeremiah."

"It's not too difficult." Noah grinned. She sipped some water and offered a drink to Mahlah. "I'm accustomed to it."

Mahlah sighed. "I'm sorry you had to find out about this night from Abishua. I wish this day had never come to pass." She swallowed the last of her drink. "Perhaps we should get back and oversee our sisters."

"Not right away. At least not for you." Noah clutched Mahlah's robe. "You need to rest. That is what I am going to tell Nemuel and the young ones while you leave camp and seek out Reuben."

"Reuben is back from battle?" Mahlah's heart sparked anew.

"Yes, victorious and unclean. He stopped me on my way into camp."

"He sought you out?" Her glee plummeted to her bruised toes.

"Don't look at me like that." Noah's expression became stern, not sisterly. "He had a message for you. Not me. Who better to bring a word to camp than someone who traipses in and out all the time?" Noah scanned the neighboring tents. "He can't return for five more days until he is clean from bloodshed."

Had Reuben thought about her while he was away at war? Mahlah walled off her heart lest it shatter again. Reuben might seek another girl for his wife. "What did he want to tell me that couldn't wait?"

A few women hurried by to collect manna.

Noah feigned a giggle. Leaning in close, she sobered. "Moses is going to count the families of Israel. War and the plague have diminished some of the clans. God wants Moses to number the fighting men."

Number the men? Mahlah's hopes diminished. She tossed her cup by the water jar and let it lay on the ramskin lip of the tent. "Our father left no sons to be counted." Did Reuben mean to forewarn her? Cool her temper so she wouldn't speak out and grumble? Like her father. "I don't care for his message."

"You most of all should care." Palms held high, Noah formed a barrier in front of her. "Our soldiers have taken cities and land. Land, Mahlah!"

"But I am not a son or a soldier. Neither are you." And she had seen firsthand Nemuel's disregard for the women in their clan. He had rejoiced over Jonah's healing, not his daughter's.

A storm wind released from Noah's mouth. "Go to Reuben and ask him yourself about Moses' decree. The fighting men of Manasseh are stationed near our livestock." Noah tipped her head in the direction of her field.

A throb boomed between Mahlah's temples. Conversing with Reuben rekindled feelings she had pressed down for years. But Reuben had always been kind to her. Was he being kind now? Was there more to his message that she did not understand? *Reuben, don't cast me a fool.*

"Won't the men be wearing loincloths?" She bit her lip at the thought of finding Reuben in a mass of scantily-clad men.

Noah clapped a hand on Mahlah's shoulder. "I have faith in you, sister. Your wisdom and bravery saved Hoglah and our relatives. If you are worried,"— Noah winked—"take one of father's cloaks and a blindfold."

She would need more than a blindfold to suppress her feelings. When Reuben was present, the air and her body warmed like a brick oven.

# 17

Twitch. Twitch. Twitch. Mahlah's eyelid drooped. Of all the times to have a spasm. She needed keen eyesight to spy out Reuben in a crowd of battle-weary men. She shouldn't complain. Because of the success of her clansmen and her people, there were new cities and new land to occupy. But the stain of blood meant seven days outside of the camp in custom with God's laws on cleanness.

Mahlah cradled her father's cloak in one hand and held her eye open with the other. Sheep bleated and scattered as she stomped through their fields. She avoided Eli and Jeremiah's areas. They may whisper about why she'd wandered from her family.

Passing a neighbor's herds, she slowed her steps and gawked. On the far outskirts, men lounged against trees and rocks, lazily conversing in small groups. Some lay on mats trying to sleep in the shade, their skin mostly bare. Legs sprawled from beneath blankets strung for temporary shelter.

Breathing deep, Mahlah coughed. With so many men and so much dirt, the air hung heavy with dust. Her nerves screamed for her to whip around and run.

Reuben would not have sought Noah if his message wasn't important. Surely, he knew the counting of men would upset her, so why did he feel the need to share Moses' decree?

"God give me strength."

Unfurling her father's robe, she held it over her head to shade her face and so as not to be easily recognized by her kin.

"I seek Reuben *ben* Nemuel." She lowered her voice to sound like a man and forced the words from her mouth. Her summons carried over the mumblings of the fighting men. "Of the clan of Hepher."

"Hepher?" a man echoed. He lumbered closer. He dipped his face beneath her shroud and opened his arms as if expecting an embrace. "Are we not worthy of you, woman?"

What had Noah gotten her into? She should have questioned her sister's plan. Abiding in the fields with shepherds had caused her sister to be more brazen than most women.

Mahlah pulled her father's cloak taut beneath her chin. This stranger would not get one peek at her form. "I received a message from my kinsman, Reuben ben Nemuel."

"If a woman appears, perhaps we should all send messages." His guttural laugh brought her to the attention of other loungers. "What is another day in the shade?"

Her cheeks grew hot. She came because she was summoned. She did not wander around as a harlot.

"I seek Reuben. None other." Backing away toward the washing jars, she slipped a hand under the folds of cloth and held it upon her knife.

"I'll be your Reuben."

Her pursuer did not retreat.

More men rose from their mats and joined in her humiliation.

Ears thrumming, she halted by the tallest water jar. If anyone came too close she would push the vessel over and drench their feet in mud.

Drawing to her full height, she whirled her father's cloak in the air. These men would see her strength. *Oh, please Lord; let these men see my weapon.*

"I am a daughter of the clan of Hepher. I seek Reuben, son of Nemuel." Her throat burned from her declaration. "Tell me where my neighbor lies."

The growing group of men cast glances at one another. One shrugged. A few chuckled.

Footfalls came from behind the tall jars.

The hair on her arms stood at attention. She whirled around, bracing for an attack.

"Mahlah?"

"Reuben?" Her heart skipped and plummeted to her belly. "Praise God. It is you."

And it was him. Bare chested with muscles etched into his arms. A wave of desire surged through her body. To be held in those arms, against that chest. Her knees grew limp.

*Stop those thoughts.*

*Don't faint. Not here. Not among these warriors.*

She threw her father's cloak over her head and perched there in the middle of unclean fighting men, shrouded like a nervous bride. Better to seem mad than to be sinful.

"We do not need witnesses to our words. Go back to your rest." The command in Reuben's voice sent a cool stream swirling through her veins.

The shuffling of sandals stirred the ground.

"Now go!"

Her knees nearly buckled. Never had she heard Reuben be so forthright and forceful. She prayed he would not set his fury upon her for her arrival.

"Mahlah, what brings you out of camp?"

His voice did not hold the wrath from moments ago. He spoke in his calm manner, a manner that had drawn her heart to him as they had come of age.

Withdrawing the cloak so she could see, she beseeched herself to look only at Reuben's eyes. Nothing else. Solely the eyes. Eyes she could picture even after he married another.

"I came—"

"It's Jonah? My son." Horror filled his face. He reached out to her, stopping before he made her unclean.

"No, it's not." She shook her head, so he would see her earnestness. "Jonah is fine now."

"Now? What do you mean?" His gaze bore into her like a starving vulture assessing its prey.

How much should she tell him? All of it? About the pit and his sister? The plague in his tent? This wasn't the time. Not when he was confined to the outskirts, left to worry for days.

"He had a fever, but Jonah is well now. He was complaining of hunger when I left."

"So, you were with him?" He stepped backward, his hand massaging his brow.

Her heart ached. She wanted to always be with him. With Jonah. Her life was somehow fuller with their smiles.

"Yes, I was with him. But that is not why I am here."

"You wished to bring me a cloak?" He glanced at the garment wrapped around her shoulders.

"Only if you need it."

He shook his head. "It would be unclean if I wore

it." His dark eyes softened. "It was your father's?"

She nodded. "That's why I am here. You sent word with Noah about a counting. That Moses is going to count the fighting men of Israel."

"Yes. God has blessed us. We have conquered cities. Walled cities with land aplenty." Excitement sped his words. "Our livestock can graze on a thousand new hills."

"What about my livestock? The flocks of Zelophehad? Will my sisters and I be given some of those hills?"

Reuben rubbed a hand over his stubbled chin.

"After Moses counts the fighting men, the leaders of each clan will assign land." Reuben's forehead ridged. "Larger families will receive more land. The head of each family will draw lots for their piece to settle."

He was babbling, reciting what the elders had been told. What he had probably heard from others as he waited to be made clean from war. Her muscles drew taut.

"You don't believe your father will put my family name in to draw lots?" There she said it. No need for a mysterious message.

"What man would?"

"You, perhaps?"

His mouth opened and closed, but he did not utter an affirmation.

Her cheeks tingled with warmth. And pain. As if someone had slapped her; Reuben's silence was a slap all its own.

"So," her voice strained in her throat. "The name of my father is as dead and buried as he. That is the message you were so eager for me to hear? Families will be counted but not mine."

At her near shriek, a man dipped a ladle in a water jar and hurried away.

"Mahlah."

Her name came from his lips, soft and gentle. It almost soothed her trembling hands like a soft caress. Almost.

He stepped closer.

"I only wanted you to be aware of what was happening, so you could be ready."

"To do what? Challenge your father and my clan?" She wrapped the cloak in a ball so tight against her belly, it pained her stomach.

Reuben's eyelashes fluttered. "There are other ways to get land."

"Wait." Her response floated in the air between them, long, and lingering. "You want me to marry off my sisters?" Tears pulsed behind her eyes. "This isn't about counting my family because my sisters won't be counted. Not as a family." Her fingers trembled. A flash of drenching him with water from the jars crossed her vision.

"If they had husbands, they would have land and protection." He bent low, hands open. "Consider it. That is all I ask. They will eventually marry."

Biting her lip, she beheld him with a wariness she had never felt before. Where was the boy who'd watched over her? Who showed kindness when her own father did not have a tiny drop to spare? Her mind taunted her. *He did not offer to protect you.*

"Of all our people, I reasoned I could trust you." She could not keep the disbelief from her chastisement. "Noah and Hoglah are old enough to consider an offer of marriage, but what about Milcah and Tirzah? What of them? Who will look out for the needs of girls with no land and no father? Shall I hand them off to someone who desires a larger family to count? May it never be."

"I did not mean to upset you." He scraped a hand over his shoulder-length hair.

Not a twinge of attraction budded in her belly. Her woeful lust had been stamped upon and tattered.

"My father may have grumbled against God, but he believed in our God and taught his daughters to do the same. The daughters of Zelophehad will be counted among the clan of Hepher. As. A. Family."

She turned and whipped her cloak over her shoulder. A few men dodged from her path.

"If that were possible, I would hope for it. Truly, I would." Reuben's shout followed after her.

Why did she have to be fond of him? Why couldn't God have brought another man into her life? But then what man would want the burden of providing for several unwed sisters? Reuben meant well with his message, but she refused to take his counsel. She had promised her mother that she would watch over her sisters, and she would not break that vow. Ever. Even if her sisters were overlooked in an official counting.

She and her sisters would carry her father's name into the Promised Land. Part of Canaan would belong to Zelophehad's offspring. She had vowed as much to her mother, and to herself.

And she would not break her own vow.

# 18

Mahlah plodded back to camp avoiding where her family's livestock roamed. She did not want to be questioned about where she had been or with whom she'd talked. Talked. She laughed. Reuben had received her truth in shouts. She hoped Eli was still entrusted with the care of their animals and that Noah ruled their tent. How was it possible that her clansman had wandered off to worship a foreign god, yet he could inherit land? She and her sisters served the God of Abraham faithfully, and yet they had no right to assume their father's portion of land.

She perched atop a rock on a hill a fair distance from the tents of Manasseh. How vast her tribe seemed to be, nestled alongside the other tribes of Israel. A sea of tent tops covered the ground. A testament to the strength of the eldest son of Joseph, a ruler over Egypt. She blinked in awe. What standing did five orphaned girls have among so many families?

The sun baked her head covering. A drip of sweat slid down the side of her nose and settled on her lip. Salt sizzled on her tongue. The weight of her father's cloak burdened her arm. She should have left it in their tent. Little good it did her to seek out Reuben. All he sought was betrothals for her sisters. He did not speak one word about her own betrothal. At least, not with him. Somehow, after their meeting, he did not seem so ruggedly handsome.

Her future, and that of her sisters, overflowed with uncertainty. Being the firstborn of Zelophehad left her with little standing in her clan. The elders of her tribe were set to scatter her sisters into different tents. Some as wives and others as servants.

Mahlah tipped her chin toward a bright blue sky. Her chest tightened, making breaths difficult. "I don't have a mother or a father, God? But you know that. You know the truth."

Tears seeped from her eyes and streaked down her cheeks. She didn't bother to brush them away.

"How can I honor the vow I made to my mother when no one will let me? I am nothing in the elders' eyes now that my father is dead."

A wisp of a cloud drifted overhead.

"Are You listening, Lord? I've seen Your cloud over the Tent of Meeting. Your pillar of fire leading our people." She swallowed, her throat thick and raw. "I saw Moses lifting a serpent on a stick so Your people would be saved. Or could be saved." She shook the images of her father's bloated body from her vision. "I know You care."

She glanced around to make sure no one had witnessed this spectacle of a girl talking to a cloud. Hadn't she already stirred the curiosity of the fighting men waiting outside the camp?

"I am not a son, but I swear I love You more than some who wear a loincloth." She hiccupped as the tears flowed. "Help me, Lord. I am pushed aside while my family is forgotten."

Did the sky brighten? A ray of light broke free from the small cloud and illuminated the ground at her feet. Were her eyes playing tricks on her? She blinked.

Another ray of light burst from the cloud.

"God? Is that You?"

Dropping to her knees, she flung her father's cloak over the rock and lifted her arms toward the blinding light. She closed her eyes and allowed the warmth to heat her flesh.

"O God of Abraham, Isaac, and Jacob, hear my prayer. I am a woman without husband or standing or means. My mother and father are gone." Her chest heaved, choking her petition. "Who is going to take care of me and my sisters?"

*I Am.*

Mahlah's eyes flew open. Someone had spoken. Had Reuben followed her?

She whipped around, but no man stood anywhere near her.

It couldn't have been? Could it?

The cloud hovered overhead in an expanse of endless sky. Her soul emptied of sorrow and soared like a skylark breaking free from the white mass and darting toward the heavens.

"What am I to do, Lord? I love my sisters. They can be brash and silly, but I love them with all my heart. We're a family." She licked her lips, warmed by the sun's rays. "God are You truly listening?"

*I Am.*

Again. She heard it.

That voice.

Forehead to dirt, she bowed. Heart racing. "Toda raba, Lord. Give me Your wisdom."

She stayed low to the ground until her back cooled and her limbs stopped trembling. She glanced at the blue hues above her. The cloud had vanished.

Leaping to her feet, she hurried toward her family's tent. She fled past women weaving and cooking without giving a glance or a greeting. Not a word would she share about her encounter at the rock. Some of her people already thought her half-mad for chastising an elder and throwing his gold into the fire.

As she neared her tent, the one with the slight tilt, her sisters' voices drifted out to her. She stilled and listened over the boom of her heart.

"I should never have slept outside this tent," Hoglah said. "My bones are still weary from the fever."

Mahlah bit her lip. *Oh, Hoglah.*

"Do not tell Mahlah." Hoglah's tone sharpened.

"She has other worries at the moment." Noah's voice held a tease.

*Don't tell them, Noah.*

"Someone help me find all my rocks," Tirzah complained. "Milcah kicked them into the corner."

"I did not." Ire filled Milcah's defense.

Hand to her mouth, Mahlah stifled her tears. This was her family. The family she'd vowed to watch over.

She beheld a slice of sky visible between the tent tops.

"God of Israel, I cannot disappoint my sisters and my mother. If what I heard today was You, then give me strength to speak to the one who speaks for You." She closed her eyes and smiled. A sack of grain weighed on her heart as her sisters' complaints and conversing filtered from the tent.

Nemuel and the leaders of Manasseh would not separate her family. Not while her lungs held breath. The daughters of Zelophehad would carry their father's name into the land God had promised His people.

She and her sisters would go above their tribal elders and seek the man who spoke to God and for God.

For a future together, she and her sisters would seek Moses.

What was one more family scandal?

# 19

In hopes of catching a word of when the leaders of Israel would gather, in the coming days, Mahlah sauntered along the Tabernacle curtain listening to gossip and quarrels. She and her sisters would seek out Moses at the assembly when witnesses abounded to hear Moses' wisdom.

Was she foolish to approach Moses in front of God's appointed overseers? What if the voice she thought she'd heard wasn't from God? What if the sky had brightened all on its own? She clasped her arms around her waist and strolled toward the tents of Moses and his nephew, Eleazar, the priest. If she and her sisters had any hope of staying together and carrying her father's name into the new lands, they would need a blessing from God's spokesman.

A group of Levites headed in her direction. Would they know of an assembly? They took care of God's house. She let the Tabernacle servants pass. Turning to follow, she came nose to neck with Reuben. A fully-clothed Reuben. A man who had disregarded her claim to land. She drew to her full height so they were almost eye to eye.

Reuben's face was void of his customary smile.
*And how do you fare this morning, Mahlah?*

"You didn't tell me the fever Jonah suffered was due to the plague. Wasn't I due the truth about my son?"

How dare he greet her with an accusation. She breathed deep to halt a hasty response. The smoke from the Tabernacle offerings filled her nostrils. The ashen scent did nothing to calm her anger; it only irritated her nose.

"I gave you the truth." She would not allow him to sully her reputation, not when she needed to be held in high regard before the assembly. "I answered your question with enough knowledge so you would not worry. Jonah's fever had broken when I left camp. The plague's hold on your family's tent was no more."

"Thanks to you."

His statement lacked the customary praise one would expect for saving another's family. But she would not take the credit.

"Thanks to God."

He widened his stance and crossed his arms. A blue-corded tassel splayed over his tunic. His face filled with wrinkles.

"Basemath told me about the idol worship."

She admired the weave of the curtain beside her, tracing the scarlet threads with her eyes and leaving Reuben to wait for her response.

"Your sister was too drunk to join in the worship." She turned her attention back to him and forced a bland expression. "I believe our kinsman Eli is to blame for her state."

"You are the one who went after her." He emphasized her role with a hint of castigation.

"I went after Hoglah." She allowed her bond with her sister to hang in the smoke-hazed air between them. "With a proper escort," she added. "And if I hadn't seen the image of their pagan god, I wouldn't have been able to banish your sister's armlet to the fire pit."

"You threw my mother's gold into the fire as well." His arms fell to his sides. "So, I've heard."

Ah, now that the illness had passed, his father must be fuming at his charred wealth. And who better to slander than the unwed girl with no father.

"I couldn't be certain your sister wasn't generous with her tainted baubles."

"My sister? Generous?" He cracked that endearing smile.

Her body readied to leap into his embrace. Traitor. Though, he had tried to warn her about the counting. He must have been fatigued from battle.

"I don't know how I would have survived the grief of losing my son." His eyes glistened. "I wouldn't have been able to enter camp to bury him. How could I have left his body to decay in this heathen land if we were called to march?"

She banished any thoughts or images of Jonah's lifeless body. Her heart ached for the briefest of moments, for she had left her father's body to decompose in pagan soil.

"He brings me joy, too." She swallowed, hard. Thinking of Jonah caused her to grin despite his father's questioning. "And worrying about him for days, well, I didn't want you to despair."

Reuben nodded, his eyes all the more captivating with tears ready to overflow.

"After all, I told you I would watch over him, and you know how stubborn I can be." She cocked her head, knowing he agreed with her assessment.

He laughed. With a sniffle, he said, "I promised Jonah he could visit your tent later. My father and I must take our places at the assembly."

An invisible horn blasted in her ear. Her brain cleared of all their chatter.

"Has Moses called a meeting of the tribal leaders?"

"Tonight. He wants Eleazar to bless the lots cast for land." Reuben turned toward the intense colors of the curtain as if noticing the location of the Tabernacle for the first time. "Father wants me to make an offering for our tribe before the prayers this evening."

"How wise." She cast a glance at the cloud covering their place of worship. This meeting with Reuben did not happen by chance. Those wisps of white meant God was with her people. With her. Right now.

*I Am.*

Her heart rallied, quaking her clothing. "I best not keep you from your duty."

He turned toward the entrance. "You're always thinking of others, Mahlah."

Oh, Reuben. If he only knew.

Tonight, she would be thinking solely of the daughters of Zelophehad and claiming their rightful inheritance.

# 20

Mahlah raced through the tents of the Levites to the tents of the tribe of Manasseh. She and her sisters would attend the assembly tonight and seek justice for their family. Her father had grumbled at the desert's harsh conditions and bland food, but he believed in God. The blood of her grandfather, Hepher, ran through her father's veins, and that same blood ran through hers. She and her sisters should be able to carry their father's name, the firstborn son of Hepher, into the Promised Land. Woe to any man who uttered the same insult as Reuben and suggest she marry off her sisters outright.

Rounding onto the wide path, she spied Noah passing Susanna's tent.

"Sister." She tugged Noah toward their dwelling. "We must have a family meeting. I saw Reuben at the Tabernacle."

"Was he dressed this time?" Noah smirked. "You have been coy about the true meaning of his message."

"I did not care for his message, but I believe he has helped us without knowing it."

"The household of Nemuel help us?" Noah sputtered a laugh. "You have been in the desert too long. Save Susanna, they have rarely shown us

115

kindness. Where was Nemuel's praise after you saved his family from the plague?"

Mahlah pushed Noah into the cooking courtyard, distracting the rest of her sisters. "It will all be different soon."

"This I must hear." Noah snatched a manna cake from a nearby basket.

"Hey. I just made those," Hoglah protested.

"Then they'll be hot." Noah bit into the cake. "Besides, Mahlah has called a meeting, so I cannot wander elsewhere."

"A meeting? For all of us?" Tirzah asked.

"Yes, but not out here." Mahlah scanned the path. Praise be, women were intent on their duties and not on their orphaned neighbors. "Slowly, go inside the tent."

Milcah helped Hoglah remove the last of the ground manna cakes from the heated stone.

Noah picked up Tirzah and playfully carried her into the tent.

Sauntering inside last, Mahlah pulled the tent flaps taut. She motioned for her sisters to gather and sit in the center of their home.

"There will be an assembly this evening." She knelt next to Hoglah. "Moses is going to bless the lots that will determine the plot of land each family is given."

Noah's expression grew serious. "Has Nemuel agreed to give us father's portion?"

"No, he has not." Mahlah pressed her lips together. How would her sisters take the coming news? "He wants me to find husbands for you and Hoglah."

"Ugh." Noah sounded as though she had ingested

spoiled meat. "Where is his loyalty?"

Hoglah hugged her knees and rocked forward. Shadows nested under her eyes.

"What about us?" Milcah grasped Tirzah's hand. "Who would we live with if you all are married?"

"You would live with me. No one has mentioned a husband for me."

She pushed away the nag of regret and wrapped her arms around Noah and Hoglah.

"We need not worry about the leaders' demands. I have a plan to keep us all under this sagging tent top. Tonight, we are going to the assembly as the daughters of Zelophehad, and we will petition Moses for father's land. God has put it upon my heart to seek Moses' wisdom. Aren't we as valuable as sons?"

"In our clan, more so." Noah slapped the ground in the middle of the small circle where they sat. "I am going with Mahlah to the assembly. We need land for our herds and flocks to grow."

"And our rocks." Tirzah laid her hand on Noah's.

"I'm going. This is the only tent I want to be in." Hoglah placed her hand on top of her sisters' hands. "I was silly to believe that taking care of it didn't matter."

"Don't leave me behind." With both hands, Milcah reached into the circle.

"Praise be." Mahlah's chest swelled bigger than the ramskin walls. "We must put on our finest robes and hold our heads high as we address our leaders."

Her sisters scrambled to rise

Tirzah nibbled her fingernail. "What if they don't give us land?"

What if they didn't? The elders of Manasseh would blame her for humiliating them in front of all the tribal elders. Her stomach twirled faster than those

Midianite dancers.

"We must trust God to act. Are we not orphans? Five of them? Does God not expect our leaders to care for the orphan and the widow?" She prayed the vision she'd beheld in the clouds was not due to the strain of the past few Sabbaths. No one had been around to utter the words she had heard that day. "We are right to ask for father's inheritance so we can remain a family and so his name will be remembered. Moses will be fair in his judgment. Our tribal elders will listen to him."

"Will Moses listen to us?" Hoglah's question dribbled with doubt.

Mahlah embraced her middle sister. "It doesn't matter. God is listening."

# 21

Back and forth inside their tent, Mahlah paced. "God of Jacob, give me wisdom. Is this what You would have Your servant do? I see no other way to save my sisters and carry my family name into Canaan, Your Promised Land." Sweat pooled above her lip. "Cast out the tremble from my limbs, for my legs do not want to march me into a meeting of men."

Milcah flung open the tent flap. "Nemuel and Reuben are leaving for the assembly. It won't be long now."

"Come." Mahlah unfolded an alabaster-colored veil. "We need to change your head covering. We must all be a sight to behold."

"That is the same color as mine." Tirzah shifted her covering as if it was somehow tainted because of the similarity to her sister's veil. Her bottom lip plumped.

"You can wear mine." Noah removed her veil. "The scarlet edging will match your cheeks."

"You don't mind changing?" Tirzah asked.

"Not at all." Noah secured the ruby fringed covering on her young sister.

Hoglah shook out her robe. "Noah could wear a rag on her head, and still all the men's eyes would turn toward her."

"Says the girl in the indigo weave who is as eye-catching as any woman in camp."

Hoglah blushed at Noah's compliment.

"No more fussing." Mahlah wished her words did not sound so weary, but if she did not force herself to leave their tent in the next breath, she might be tempted to squabble all night. "We need to pray and ask God to open Moses' heart to our plight."

"Shouldn't we pray for all the leaders' hearts to be open?" Milcah cast a glance at her sisters.

Milcah was correct once again.

"We shall." Mahlah grasped Milcah's hand. "Nothing is too hard for our God. He has felled kingdoms and given us walled cities to live in. He can change a man's beliefs."

Noah sighed. "Pray, Mahlah, before our knees buckle from all our woes."

"God of Abraham, Isaac, and Jacob; You are the father to the fatherless. Soften the hearts of the elders to our plea. May we inherit land in our father's name, so we can stay together as a family."

"God of Jacob, hear our prayer." Noah cast a glance in Mahlah's direction and nodded.

Noah's support was a fresh dip of water.

"May it be so." Mahlah finished the prayer with a mouth as dry as withered reeds.

"Can I close my eyes in the assembly?" Tirzah winked one eye then the other.

"Only when we are standing still." Noah scrubbed a hand over Tirzah's head covering.

"Stop." Tirzah ducked and ran into Mahlah.

"Shhh." Her sister's playful banter echoed in Mahlah's head. Didn't they realize the seriousness of this night? After her request for land, the men may shout their contempt or hurl insults. Worse still would be if they hurled rocks. *Protect us, God.*

Before Mahlah left their tent, she untied her belt and left her knife wrapped in her sleeping mat. God would be her defender tonight, not the blade bestowed upon her by her father.

Mahlah ushered her sisters out of their home and led them away from Nemuel's tent and through alleys toward the Tabernacle. As they neared the center of camp, Jonah came bounding around a corner followed by Basemath. Why were they near the tents of the Levites?

"Mah-lah." Jonah tugged on her robe wanting to be held.

If only she could resist those big eyes and chubby cheeks. She bent and lifted Jonah, settling him on her hip.

"Pretty." He fingered her mustard-hued veil.

"You look like a bride." Basemath sauntered closer, her gaze scanning the line of girls.

"And we are in a hurry like one." Mahlah's answer held a not-so-subtle warning that she would not explain about their appearance.

A few men hastened by on their way toward the Tabernacle.

Basemath's brow furrowed. "My father is attending a gathering before the Tent of Meeting. Moses is going to bless the lots."

"Yes, he is." Noah wrapped her arms around Jonah and removed him from Mahlah's grasp. "We must borrow Mahlah for this eve. She will visit your tent soon."

"Soon," Jonah repeated.

"Come now." Basemath clasped the boy's hand. "We must sup."

Food was the farthest thing from Mahlah's thoughts. Her stomach pained as if it were full of jagged rocks. She waved to Jonah. The boy's joyous, energetic smile bore into her burdened heart.

When Basemath glanced over her shoulder, Mahlah glimpsed a wetness in her eyes. That would be a first. Her neighbor usually rejoiced when others cried, except after the plague. Now, she rarely spoke and remained close to home.

"Mahlah," Basemath began. "I wish my father would value me like a son."

"I wish that for all of us." Mahlah rolled her shoulders, trying to release a pinch in her neck.

"Then go." Basemath sniffled. "Why do you tarry?"

Pressure to the small of Mahlah's back urged her along.

"Do not mention you saw us." Noah wrapped an arm around Mahlah's shoulders. "We don't need an overseer tonight."

Basemath nodded. "I won't."

Mahlah needed her headstrong sister more than ever. Marching toward the Tabernacle, she didn't know how one sandal passed in front of the other. This camp she had grown up in, with its rows of tents and cooking fires, seemed foreign. Her parents no longer roamed these paths, neither her grandparents. Why did her sisters' well-being have to be championed by an unmarried orphan?

Nearing the entrance to the Tabernacle, she slowed her steps. Through the opening in the colorful curtain, she could see Moses standing before the tent where the

Ark of the Covenant rested. Thick and white, the cloud of God hung above the holy place. She swallowed, but no saliva moistened her throat.

Elders and leaders, man after man, faced Moses; his fellow leader, Joshua; and Eleazar, God's favored priest. The scarlet, purple, and blue threads of the tapestry walls could not compete with the stones and jewels sewn into the priest's ephod. Eleazar was a tower of blue, gold, and gems. Mahlah's mustard veil, worn by her mother on her wedding day, was but a scrap of cloth compared to the magnificence of Eleazar's robe.

As she shuffled closer to the leaders of Israel, men turned to see who dared stroll to the front of the gathering. The growl of male voices hushed. A low rumble of mutterings began. Mumblings about her and mumblings about her father.

Her toe struck stone. A throb of pain filled her foot.

Twitch. Twitch. Twitch. Not her eye, too?

"I don't know if I can do this."

"Yes, you can, Daughter of Zelophehad," Noah whispered. "You are the strongest woman I know, and we are all here behind you."

Her sisters echoed Noah's belief.

Mahlah rallied her spirit and strode boldly toward the leader of Israel even though her mouth tasted of salt and blood.

*God of Abraham, Isaac, and Jacob give me Your strength.*

# 22

The last time Mahlah was this close to Moses was when her father lay dying. If only her father had glimpsed the serpent Moses had held high, this matter of inheriting land would have been settled. Her father would have drawn lots for a portion alongside his brothers. Being the firstborn son of Hepher, he would have received a double portion of land. Now she had to ask for something that had never been granted before. She had to ask for an inheritance, and daughters did not inherit land among the tribes of Israel.

Nemuel stalked toward the narrow aisle she and her sisters strode. His sandals crushed anyone's feet who did not clear his path.

She scanned the crowd for Reuben, but he did not follow his father.

*Set your eyes upon Moses. He speaks for God.*

"What is the meaning of this display?" Nemuel flipped his ringed fingers at her sisters. "Women do not belong at this assembly. Leave at once before you bring ridicule upon our clan."

"Our father attended these meetings." Mahlah forced each syllable through her parched throat. "I am seeing to my sisters' well-being. We are the daughters of Zelophehad. We stand before everyone here as a testimony to our father's lineage. Our future needs consideration, so we are here to seek our father's portion of land."

Her elder scoffed. "How are you different from any other woman in this camp? If you desire land, then I will arrange a betrothal." He lunged to grasp her arm. "Leave here at once."

She dodged Nemuel's fat fingers as Noah blocked their leader's advance.

Mahlah removed her sandal and held it high above her embroidered head covering. She demanded a hearing with the leather that bound her foot. She had business to transact in this assembly. The business of a birthright.

She glanced at the closest gawkers. "We have come in earnest to claim land."

Men gasped.

"You are mad or drunk." Nemuel reached for her hair.

She sidestepped his attack.

"Remove yourself and return to your tent." Elders closed in, their fists beating the air.

Noah and Hoglah gathered the young ones and stood back to back.

*Slap. Slap.* Mahlah beat her sandal against her palm. *Slap. Slap.*

The clop dulled in the dampness of her skin, but she would not retreat. She was the eldest daughter of Zelophehad. A daughter with no mother or father. An orphan. She had a right to be heard among God's people and discuss her claim to land.

"My sisters and I are due an inheritance. We are orphaned daughters of the Most High."

"Do you want to be struck down?" Nemuel's hot breath swarmed her senses.

A long-nosed elder wielded a stone. She darted toward Moses, elbowing anyone who dared reach for her robe.

"Moses." she shrieked. "I beseech you. Hear our plea."

"Enough." Nemuel clawed at the back of her neck. His fingernails found flesh. "Curse you and your stubbornness."

Skin stinging, she bent her knees and let her weight drop toward the trodden soil. Sandal in hand, and hunched like a child, she crawled toward Moses' feet.

Moses raised the staff in his hand. "Let her speak."

"But, my lord, she has no standing here." Nemuel glanced at Eleazar, dressed in his finery. "This matter should be decided by our clan not in an assembly."

Agreement echoed throughout the crowd.

"Cease your complaining," Joshua cried out.

Her challengers hushed at the rebuke.

"This woman has brought the matter to the assembly. It will not burden us to hear it." Leaning on his staff, Moses nodded for her to begin.

She cleared her throat and prayed her voice did not fail. Giving a brief nod of respect to Nemuel, she bowed and fixed her full attention on Moses, Joshua, and Eleazar.

"My sisters and I are the daughters of Zelophehad, from the clan of Hepher, a descendant of Manasseh, eldest son of our forefather Joseph." She allowed the names of her ancestors to rest on the ears of the elders. "Should such a lineage be lost as we enter the land promised by our God?"

A man pushed through the onlookers and stationed himself at Nemuel's side.

Reuben! Would he be a voice of reason? He alone warned her about the counting of the fighting men. Oh, to have an ally in this place.

"We have come together to bless the lots." Reuben spoke as if he was the overseer of the tribes. "But we are not drawing them this eve. Surely, the clan of Hepher can see to this request when the land is divided." Reuben gave her a reassuring nod.

Did he expect his comments to be a balm?

Her cheeks grew hot. Reuben's betrayal hummed in her ears. His father, and their clansmen, would never agree to her demands.

She stepped closer to Moses, her back to her clan's leaders.

"If my sisters and I are not given consideration this eve, then my father's name will not be counted among the lots."

Another tribal elder shot to his feet. "Women cannot inherit land. This is nonsense."

"Silence these girls, Nemuel," another shouted.

Mahlah turned, breathed deep, squared her shoulders, and pointed her sandal at the closest men. If she wielded a sword, she would have pierced their robes. "My father deserves to be remembered among his brothers and among his clan."

"Your father cursed God." Nemuel roared his rebuke. "His body rots in the desert."

She rocked backward, her bones unsteady. Her elder's retort haunting her soul. "Hush your words." A storm wind whirled inside Mahlah's chest.

Tirzah began to cry.

"My…" Mahlah hesitated. "Our father grumbled

at the hardship of life in the desert, but he still worshiped our God. A God we have remained faithful to in our wandering." Mahlah turned toward Reuben as a witness to her testimony. "If what I say is true, then say it is so. Are you not our neighbor?"

Reuben might as well have been a wood carving. He didn't utter one defense of her father. Or her.

Twitch. Twitch. Tiny tremors wracked her eyelid.

She blinked away the weakness. She would stand here even if she were deaf, dumb, and blind and fight for her sisters' future.

"Someone, remove these girls," a man yelled.

Chants raised in assent.

Mahlah beheld the gray-bearded leader of her people. Moses' warm brown eyes held her gaze as if he remembered her tear-choked pleas over her father's dying body. The leader's face, etched with sunbaked grooves, bestowed on her the dignity of an invited guest. He lifted his staff, and the jeers rising from the crowd quieted like a brief rain.

Eleazar, sullen in expression, cast a bewildered glance at Moses. The priest remained closed-lipped, deferring to his uncle.

Mahlah slung her fancy mustard-hued covering over her shoulders. *Mother, I am honoring my vow.*

"Leader," she began. "You heard my father's charges. God did not have the ground swallow him alive like others who questioned God. My father paid for his transgressions with his life. But my sisters and I are a wellspring of belief. We hold to the ways of God." Mahlah turned and swept an arm in the direction of her sisters, their staunch line now curved and held together by comforting arms. "Behold the faithful heirs of Zelophehad."

"Get out." Nemuel grabbed her arm with such ferocity, her hand numbed.

"Unhand her," Moses demanded.

"'Father." Reuben's plea muffled amidst the cheers and shouts of the assemblymen.

Moses whacked his wooden staff near Nemuel's toes. "Fall back. This woman seeks an answer to her request from the One True God."

"You aren't going to grant her request?" Nemuel's tone all but condemned their leader's consideration.

Reuben put a hand of restraint upon his father.

Moses pounded his staff. "It is not for me to decide. The land is God's to give. Are we not here to pray for His guidance? God's ways are not always our ways. I will seek His counsel on behalf of the firstborn of Zelophehad."

*Lord, grant my request. Spare us any retaliation.*

"But they are girls." Nemuel appealed to his fellow leaders. "Men are stewards of the land. These girls have not fought for a single ditch. Upright men have felled our enemies. Not upright women."

Reuben's gaze had not found hers since he had reined in his father's anger. Her heart sank a little lower in her chest. What if God looked favorably upon her and Reuben did not?

"Women are stewards of our land." Fist to hip, Noah approached their uncle. "Do I not tend to our livestock? Have not the births of our lambs and kids been double that of the men in our clan?"

Nemuel balked. "Because of your cousins' skill. Not of your own."

"That is folly." Noah rounded on the crowd and returned their scowls.

"Silence." Moses raised his staff and held it above

her kin. "Stop this bickering. I will bring the matter before God."

"But they have no standing." Nemuel scrubbed a hand across his forehead nearly dislodging his turban.

"There is no harm in petitioning God," Reuben said. "Were we not going to ask Him to bless the lots in distribution of the land?"

Finally, a hint of an ally.

"My own son speaks nonsense." Clicking his tongue, her elder addressed the men standing nearby. "Why not give land to all the women in this camp? Isn't that what these girls desire?"

A crowd of elders sealed off the center aisle, barricading her sisters from leaving. Their angry shouts heaped disdain on her family name.

Mahlah's right eye fluttered. The mass of men surrounding her made her feel like bread baking on a slab of stone. Sweat trickled down the side of her face.

She bowed her head to Moses and said, "We do not mean any disrespect to our elders. My sisters and I want to honor our father's name. We will accept whatever God decrees. May God grant you wisdom in considering our request."

Milcah eased forward. Her amber-brown eyes appeared too big for her slim face. A strong gust of wind could have blown her sister into the crowd.

"When will you talk to God about us?" Milcah's eyes blinked as she faced Moses. "It is getting rather loud."

Moses pursed his lips and cast a glance at Eleazar. "I believe with all the commotion in this assembly, my child, I shall approach our God in haste."

"Toda raba, my lord." Mahlah slipped her sandal onto her foot. "Shall we stay here and wait for you?"

"Do you wish to return to your tent?" Moses tipped his head toward the elders of her tribe.

She glanced above Moses at the cloud settled upon the tent where the Ark of her people waited. Where God waited between the golden cherubim in the holiest of places. Her God was waiting mere feet away. She breathed in the smoke from the many campfires tainting the air. Staring at the cloud overhead, she remembered the warm rays of sun and the comforting voice she thought she had heard when she prayed by the rock. Her tense muscles suddenly, and inexplicably, softened like pounded leather.

"I believe we'll stay here. With God."

# 23

Mahlah and her sisters huddled near the entrance to the Tent of Meeting. More men had joined the assembly, swallowing the center aisle and crowding the open spaces in front of the holy tent cared for by the priests. Men. Everywhere. Men. Squabbling. No doubt re-telling her request of Moses and raising a raucous. The stares of the leaders stationed near her sisters held no sympathy for the orphaned girls. Their mouths snarled. Their nostrils flared.

Her cheeks flamed. How dare these elders disregard her claim. Didn't the same blood that pulsed through Nemuel's veins, pulse through her body? Her bloodline heralded Joseph, Jacob, Isaac, and Abraham.

Reuben strutted forward. He carried a waterskin and cups.

Her heart assaulted her ribs but not with the normal, pleasant flutter that accompanied Reuben's presence. Her friend had defended his father and his own station above her petition for land.

She edged away from her sisters.

Reuben thrust the waterskin into her hand. "I cannot believe you betrayed me. I sent word, so you could prepare your household, and now my father fears for his life."

Nemuel could handle a few disgruntled men. No

uprising would occur with Eleazar in his jewel-laden ephod perched outside the tent and Moses kneeling in prayer beside it.

She stiffened at the perusal of Reuben's dark eyes. No compassion glistened in his gaze.

"What did you expect me to prepare my sisters for? Servitude?"

"A customary future with a husband." Reuben dangled the cups in front of her face.

Noah reached in and grabbed a cup. "I'll take those and the skin. You two keep squabbling."

Mahlah crossed her arms and glared at the man who had always harbored a quiet wisdom.

"Have you forgotten about marriage and obedience, Mahlah? About the reputation of our clan? I could go on. But you don't seem to listen to reason anymore."

"Anymore?" She fisted her hands and fought the temptation to lash out. "In all the years you have known me, when have I been unreasonable?"

He bent low, so his breath blew in her face. "Leaving the camp in the dark of night. Strolling among unclean men. Need I go on?"

"All of that I did to take care of my sisters. And I would do it all again."

"You took on the role of an elder, of which, you are not."

"I took on the role of a firstborn, of which I am." Her voice rasped a defense.

Reuben straightened and drew away from her.

Good. At this moment, she did not want to be near him. In all her years, had she ever had that thought? She glimpsed her sisters drinking water and whispering. Her place was with them.

Turning her gaze upon Reuben, she battled any twitch threatening to mar her fierce tirade. "Where were the elders of Hepher when my father needed comfort? What elder counselled my father when frustration ruled his senses?"

"Do not blame the clan of Hepher for your father's sins. He alone led a charge against God. Your father abandoned you. His clan has remained steadfast."

"I will not abandon my sisters. I vowed to my mother to keep watch over them, and that is one vow I will uphold until I take my last breath."

Reuben beheld her like a stiff-necked elder. "Did you learn nothing from your father's disobedience?" His voice was smooth as an Egyptian's robe, but it pierced her soul.

"Yes, I did." She struggled with her answer, coaxing every syllable from her quivering lips. "I learned that God will provide for me and my sisters. Shalom." Stepping away, she turned and took the waterskin from Noah.

"I'll pour." Noah retrieved the skin. "Your hands are shaking. Too bad we don't have something stronger." Arching her eyebrows, Noah's gaze fell to Reuben's haughty stature.

"Do not worry, Sister. He is one man."

Mahlah's heart constricted. She had loved that one man since she was a child.

Before she could swallow her refreshment, Moses stood with the help of his staff and turned toward the assembly. The din of male voices hushed.

Mahlah choked and gasped for air.

"God is punishing her," a man bellowed.

Noah patted Mahlah on her back. "I never thought them such fools."

Calming her cough, Mahlah led her sisters forward. They knelt before Moses, hand in hand, a chain of orphaned girls.

"Daughters of Zelophehad," Moses called in a loud voice. He raised his staff like a scepter over the crowd. "The God of Abraham, Isaac, and Jacob has heard your plea."

Mahlah's fingers went numb where she grasped Hoglah's and Milcah's hands.

Moses scanned the assembly. "Leaders of Israel, hear these words from our God. If a man dies and leaves no son, his inheritance shall be given to his daughters."

A rush of gasps filled the stale air.

Had she heard Moses correctly? Would they receive a plot of land in their father's name? Her body felt as if it floated above the soil.

"This day," Moses continued, "the inheritance of Zelophehad, son of Hepher, shall be given to his daughters. His offspring shall inherit property among their father's relatives."

"Praise be to God." Mahlah rose, her arms outstretched toward Moses. "Thank you, my lord. My heart overflows with blessing." Her eyes moistened with joyous tears. "Praise God." She embraced her sisters with abandon.

"What good is your praise? No man will have a bold nag as a wife," a bystander shouted.

Moses stomped his staff. "Listen to God's words. If a man has no sons or daughters, his inheritance shall then go to his brothers. Or to his father's brothers. This is God's ordinance."

Head bowed, Mahlah prayed. "The Lord is my God, and I will praise Him; my father's God, and I will exalt Him."

"Praise God." Tirzah jumped to her feet and waved her hands in the air. She hopped in a circle, dancing.

"Let us rejoice in this word from God," Eleazar, the priest, pronounced. "These five women sought the counsel of the Almighty and have been rewarded for their wisdom. After a time, we will pray over the lots."

Moses closed his eyes and began reciting the *Shema.*

"Here O Israel, the Lord is our God. The Lord alone..."

Mere feet from where Moses had spoken with God, Mahlah joined her sisters arm in arm, and swayed, their head coverings askew, their mouths open wide, laughing reverently. Their future was secure.

"Love the Lord your God." *Our God.* "With all your heart and with all your soul..."

"And with all your might," Noah added.

"The name of Zelophehad will be remembered in Canaan." Tears pooled in Hoglah's eyes.

"We have been granted land." Mahlah kissed Hoglah's cheek. "We can remain a family."

She pressed her hands together and bobbed her head toward Moses, Joshua, and Eleazar. Her kinsmen, Abishua, Nemuel, Reuben, and Eli, stood shoulder to shoulder forming an unapproving wall.

Two men approached their circle.

"See. It is her. I told you." The tall, thin man elbowed the other. He opened his arms. "You do not remember us? Perhaps if I had my camel?"

"The men from the tribe of Asher," Noah whispered.

"I remember, Shuni." And she remembered the shock of finding him among her sisters. If only that pagan thief, Balaam, had not stolen their goat and distracted her. "You helped my sisters carry our load. Toda raba."

"Perhaps we shall come visit and help you cross the Jordan." Shuni rocked forward on his sandals as if he was prepared to start the journey right then and there.

"You are always welcome." Hoglah smiled at the tall Asherite.

"We should leave you men to the business of blessing lots." Mahlah gave a brief nod to Shuni and his brother. "Shalom."

She bowed to Eleazar and ushered her sisters toward the entrance to the Tent of Meeting.

Men let her family pass, but a glower of distrust followed her sisters.

God had been faithful in abundance. She had His pledge of land in an amount to support five orphaned women. Praise be.

A short distance from the gathering place, Mahlah halted. She lifted her hands toward the stars. "Let us give thanks to a God who gave wisdom to a daughter of Jacob. May He guide us into the Promised Land."

Her sisters raised their hands in praise.

Mahlah beheld a vibrant star. A star that brightened and then faded into the shadowed heavens.

# 24

Early the next morning, Mahlah lay awake facing the tent flap and remembering every harsh word spoken at the assembly. The scorn from the crowd threatened to dampen the joy of being a future landowner. How could her people condemn her boldness when God had agreed with her? The Most High had granted her the right to inherit property in her father's name.

The scuffle of sandals interrupted her thoughts. Leather slapped the path outside her tent. First one man stomped past. Then another. A woman wandering about at night would not make such noise. But were these footfalls friend or foe?

Mahlah unlaced the tent flap and peeked outside. Men were on the move, but no trumpet had sounded for the camp to march. With the moonlight and a hard squint, she recognized a distant relative from another clan of Manasseh. A sword was strapped to his hip. He wore a short tunic that suggested her people were going to war.

She glanced at her sleeping sisters and then hastily wrapped her veil over her head, flinging it around her shoulders. She emerged from her tent. Heart pounding, she jogged to catch her relative.

"Helek," she called, keeping her voice low. "Why

are you leaving camp?" Surely the scouting of land would be done during the day.

Her tribesman slowed his steps. The men beside him whispered in his ear.

"Were you too busy rejoicing over your inheritance to hear Moses' instructions?" He strode forward, passing Nemuel's tent without answering her question.

"Do you wish to go and kill the Baal worshipers with us?" His companion said, holding back a chuckle.

"She is not in the top thousand warriors." Helek angled toward the center of camp.

"Not even in the top tens of thousands."

Fine. Let them jest. Was she to be an outcast for seeking land?

Had Moses called an assembly before this battle? At least Moses would not slander her name.

"Brother," a man's voice rasped.

Mahlah stilled. She knew that deep, caress of a voice. And she did not have a sinew of strength to fight with Reuben once again.

Flexing her fingers, she tugged on her head covering so her face stayed hidden behind a drape of cloth. She shifted closer to the nearest tent and waited for the men to move on.

Reuben tapped the hilt of his sword and then slapped Helek on the back. The small band lumbered onward.

Helek spoke into Reuben's ear.

Her blood became a cool stream.

The men turned. Reuben turned. And gawked. At her.

She captured their glares. Had she not fought for her inheritance in a crowd of jeering men? Her concern for her tribe this morn was not without merit. She did not wish for her people to perish.

Reuben plodded closer to her while the men waited.

"What are you doing out at this hour?" A faint hint of concern softened the grumble of his question.

Easing from the shadows of the tent, she beheld Reuben's rugged face.

"I heard the scuffle of feet. I thought there might be an attack."

"Not on our camp." Reuben grew taller as he puffed out his chest and cast a glance at the men filing down the pathways toward the Tabernacle. "You left the assembly before Moses gave a charge to the tribes. We are to take vengeance on the Midianites for seducing our men into idol worship. The best fighting men from each tribe will do the Lord's work."

Visions of Balaam and the half-naked women clamoring for his affections, stirred her stomach.

"I want to forget what I saw in the pit." She swallowed the sour taste pooling in her throat. "Our God will not forget."

"Go home, Mahlah. War is no place for a woman."

"I know." She hugged her waist as if the night had suddenly grown cooler. "I don't mind continuing to watch over Jonah."

Helek let out a low whistle.

Reuben acknowledged their tribesman and then returned his attention to her. "Toda raba." He winked and then backed away, holding her captive with an esteemed gaze. "Remember me in your petitions to God. May I be as brave in battle as you were in the assembly."

He nodded and joined the fighting men of

Manasseh.

With a slight bob of her chin, she nodded back. Nothing wild. Nothing meek. Nothing to display the geyser of delight springing from her soul. Reuben had not been indignant or rude. He had simply been the boy who lived a tent away from her all her life. He had simply been Reuben.

And it was then, as Reuben and the men of Manasseh marched off into a swarm of tent tops, that deep in her heart she reasoned, even if it was for acquiring land, she grew weary of war.

# 25

Days later, nothing had changed, yet everything had changed. Land had been granted to her and her sisters in their father's name, but regular duties continued. The daughters of Zelophehad set to their tasks in haste and in silence as warriors trickled into camp from the battle against the Midianite seducers.

Hoisting a water jar onto her shoulder, Mahlah headed toward her tent. She wound through pathways where women and children labored. Since the assembly, Nemuel had not spoken to her. No elder of Manasseh, nor any other tribe, publicly chastised her fortitude, for no elder dared to malign Moses or their God.

Praise be.

Her own cooking courtyard brimmed with activity. Without complaint, Basemath and Hoglah stoked the small acacia wood fire. Milcah and Tirzah ground manna, heads down, wrists twisting in earnest.

Jonah jumped off a sitting stone and charged like a bull toward her legs. He reached for a lift.

"I cannot hold you with one arm," Mahlah said. "I will spill this jug of water."

"I thirsty." Jonah swiped a hand across his forehead as if sitting had been strenuous work.

Mahlah laughed. "Did your aunt and Hoglah push you into labor?" She set the jar by the tent lead.

"If only I could set that boy to a task." Basemath rose and dipped a cup for a drink. "I pray my brother hurries home from war."

"We pray for Reuben and all of our fighting men." Mahlah pressed her lips together. She did not want to remember the harsh words spoken at the assembly. How could any of the men of Israel have known what God was going to bestow upon her family? Daughters had never been granted an inheritance. Until now.

She wished to remember only the acknowledgement of her presence which Reuben had given before going off to fight. He could have ignored her and rushed off with her cousin Helek. Instead, Reuben made her believe that a few of the tattered threads in their relationship had been mended.

Jonah tugged on her robe and pointed to the basket of manna. "Bread?"

The boy's expectant thick-lashed eyes were a vision of his father's. Reuben's son not only tugged on her garment, he tugged on her heart. She took his hand. "It looks like we have enough ground for a feast."

Hoglah set the flat cooking stone over the fire. "God has blessed us abundantly this morn."

"So, it seems." Mahlah stroked Jonah's soft curls. "It won't be long. Hoglah has been busy."

Smoke from the crackling acacia wood filled Mahlah's nostrils. A grayish haze fell over the small area abutting their tent.

Three men ambled toward their cooking courtyard.

Were they to have visitors? Mahlah's pulse

quickened. What business needed discussing at this hour? Was land to be distributed to the tribes?

A young man opened his arms to her as if he were her groom. "See, what did I tell you? The daughters of Zelophehad are hard at work."

Shuni. Straight away, Mahlah recognized their friend from the tribe of Asher. "Greetings." She nodded at Shuni's brother and another man with whom she was not acquainted. Why had Shuni brought a stranger? Though she had been granted land, she did not have the standing of a male head of household in her tribe. She also did not have a brother to oversee any arranged visit. "What takes you from your herds?"

"We come with gifts from my father." Shuni held up a skin and a satchel. "Wine and melons. Both are sweet." He ticked his last syllable. "We must celebrate your blessing."

Hoglah strolled toward their visitors with a host's smile. Perhaps this wasn't business? *Abundant manna indeed.*

With a disguised lunge, Mahlah blocked her sister's sashay. She tipped her head. "And who have you brought to our tent? We have not been introduced."

"My kinsman Ehud is a fine herdsman as well." Shuni patted his cousin on the back. "His camels are well-trained."

"None are smarter." Ehud gave Mahlah a gap-toothed grin.

"I am sure." Her stomach sank. A camel trainer dressed in an unsoiled robe could only mean one thing. Ehud had come to impress her sisters. Of all the times not to have a father. Did these men not understand the perilous position they were instigating? An invitation to sup would fuel gossip among her clansmen. She had no male relatives present save Jonah. Her right to land was secure, wasn't it? God had spoken her inheritance to Moses. Moses proclaimed her right in an assembly. She had not summoned these men or broken any laws. They were in public, no less.

Hoglah stepped beside Mahlah. "Your clan's camels helped us on our march to Moab."

"Yes, indeed." Shuni shifted closer to the sitting stones.

*Please do not sit.*

Jonah wedged himself between Shuni and the nearest stone. Thank goodness hunger ruled Jonah's belly.

Basemath sneaked her nephew a small piece of bread. "Are you not needed to fight the Midianites?" She slapped another cake of moistened manna onto the stone. "I heard Moses chose men of fine standing to attack the heathens." She brushed the dough from her fingertips with loud claps. "You are still here."

Shuni's brother widened his stance. "Our strength will be needed to fell the walled cities across the Jordan. We will wield our swords like none other and overcome the land like locusts." He raised a fist as if already celebrating victory.

"You are not the only fine swordsman, brother." Shuni jostled Ehud and pretended to unsheathe a sword. "All of us have seen battle." Shuni's sandals scuffed ruts into the dirt as he feigned lunges at Ehud.

Were these suitors or playmates of Jonah's? Mahlah withdrew closer to the fire lest these silly men fall into the flames.

Ehud ax-chopped Shuni's shoulder as he

simulated a lethal blow.

Shuni dipped and clutched his chest. With swift motion, he poked an air-forged blade at his cousin.

"Me, too." Wide-eyed, Jonah climbed over a sitting stone and ran to join the lighthearted game.

Ehud leapt sideways, crushing Jonah's small sandal.

"Ow." Jonah clutched his leg and began to cry.

*Fools.* Mahlah bent to grab the boy.

Off balance, Ehud swung his arms and tried to keep himself upright.

*Whack!*

Ehud's elbow smashed into her cheek.

She plopped on her tailbone as gracefully as an overfilled sack of grain. Her face throbbed. Her pain was not imaginary like their feigned battle.

"Sister!" The shriek came from the wide path.

Noah and Jeremiah jogged to her aid. Her sister handed a skin brimming with goat's milk to Jeremiah and leaned forward to assist her.

Ehud's gaze inspected every curve of Noah's form. "Is she a daughter of Zelophehad?" His giddy grin drew Mahlah's ire.

And Jeremiah's.

Jeremiah slung the milkskin and hit Ehud in the nose.

Ehud raised a fist.

"No." Mahlah leapt to her feet. She spread out her arms and placed a hand in front of each man. She had to keep Ehud and Jeremiah apart. "There will be no fighting in this household."

"No figh-ting," Jonah echoed. The boy mimicked her with his arms stretched wide.

"What is going on here?"

*Nemuel?* Oh, no, no, no. Why now?

Mahlah's skin tingled as if she'd huddled too close to the fire. She hadn't seen her neighboring elder in days.

Turning, she clenched her teeth and let the bruising ache from Ehud's folly throb through the side of her face.

"Who are these men?" Nemuel halted a few feet from her visitors, his nose wrinkled like a prune.

No one answered.

Everyone's gaze bore into her. How could she appease an elder's wrath?

"Um." The once pleasant smoke irritated her throat. "These are the men who offered us assistance when we traveled in the desert. They were passing by our tent." True, but even a fool could see these men sought more than a casual "Shalom."

Shuni strutted forward, straightening his turban. "We come bearing gifts for—"

"Gifts! What gifts?" Nemuel's eyes bulged as if Shuni had slandered his name. "This is unacceptable. You do not belong among our tents. Where is your father's clan?"

Mahlah glanced at her sisters. They watched stone-still and thin-lipped by the fire pit. They appeared more afraid of Nemuel's arrival than when they stood before Moses and the assembly.

Hands on hips, Shuni said, "I am Shuni ben Beriah, from the Imnite clan of Asher."

"We do not answer to you." Ehud's stare strayed toward Noah.

"You will answer to me in this section of the camp." Nemuel stomped his sandal. "I am a leader of Manasseh, firstborn of Joseph, and I will seek counsel with your tribal elders if you do not leave at once."

Rubbing her temple to keep the throb in her jaw from traveling to her head, Mahlah shifted to stand alongside their leader. She had no choice. God had bestowed land on her family, but they still belonged to the clan of Hepher.

"Please," she said. "It was kind of your father to send us gifts, but I ask that you honor my elder's request. Your visit is all the blessing we need this morn." She bobbed her head and beheld the men of Asher with respect, even though they had trampled her courtyard with their raucous behavior.

Shuni back-stepped a few paces. His brow furrowed. "I've heard stories of how you beseeched Moses in the assembly. I do not see a strong woman this day. All I see is a foolish girl."

His insult hung in the air. Nemuel did not challenge it, nor did her sisters. Shuni had impaled her heart with his imaginary sword. And if that wasn't enough, he twisted the blade.

Her cheek pounded in pain. What did this man know of her strength? Had he challenged Moses and the tribal leaders in an assembly?

She stomped toward her tent and grabbed the wineskin. She shoved the skin into Shuni's chest. "I'm not thirsty." Grabbing the satchel of melons, she hurled it at Ehud and his cousin. "Nor am I hungry. Your fruit is not sweet." She made sure to tick off her last syllable and mimic her visitor. "May you leave us be. This. Day."

Shrugging, Shuni turned his back on her and urged his brother and cousin onward.

Nemuel let out a grunt of consternation. "What is the meaning of all of this commotion?"

Their elder demanded an answer regarding their visitors, but no matter what excuse she gave him, he would see what he wanted to see in the matter.

"I wish I knew." She beheld Nemuel like a trusted advisor. "We were going about our duties, and then all of a sudden, these men were fighting a fake battle."

Noah retrieved the skin of milk from Jeremiah and traipsed toward a stone near the fire. Jeremiah followed Noah like a lost lamb.

"You cannot hold Mahlah responsible for the whims of those fools." Noah settled onto a rock and began pouring milk into cups. "They were too bold to come here and cause trouble."

Nemuel tapped his foot. He glowered at the shepherdess.

Jeremiah rolled a larger stone closer to Noah.

Did Noah believe she was lounging in a pasture?

Mahlah shook her head and regretted it. Her jaw ached.

Nemuel huffed at Noah. Loudly. "Why must you interrupt? And why must you drag that lame calf of a man with you?"

"My son is not lame."

Mahlah whipped around in the direction of the deep voice. Abishua stalked toward his kinsman. Shoulders broad and arms crossed, he appeared a daunting sight.

*God, spare us another fight, real or feigned.*

"The daughter of Zelophehad you addressed has tended flocks with my son for many seasons. You agreed to the arrangement." Abishua glanced at his son. "So did Zelophehad."

Trying to match Abishua's stature, Nemuel narrowed his stance. "That girl is of marriageable age."

"I believe you have an unmarried son, as well." Abishua cocked his head. He motioned for Jeremiah to join him.

"Daughter," Nemuel shouted to Basemath. "Your mother has need of you."

Cheeks growing scarlet, Basemath wiped her hands on a cloth.

Only then did Mahlah spy Jonah with a mouth full of manna. The boy had traded imaginary battles for filling his stomach.

Veil pulled low, Basemath grabbed Jonah's hand and followed her father.

How had a calm morning turned into condemnation? Shuni came as a friend, but his insult cast him as a foe. Thankfully, Reuben was fighting the Midianites and not shadowing his father, but then she would guess he had already heard bountiful slander regarding her reputation.

Tirzah leaned against Mahlah's leg.

"I wish you had kept the melons."

# 26

Mahlah's stomach gurgled. With all the commotion and bickering, she had not eaten one morsel before Shuni and his relatives arrived. She slumped onto a sitting stone while Tirzah rambled on about melons. At least presently, no men practiced battle moves in front of her tent. She counted it a blessing that this day could only get easier.

Noah held out a cup. "Would you like some milk?"

"Please. My cheek aches, and I have spent more words than my mind had summoned this morn."

Hoglah flipped a manna cake into a basket. "Perhaps you should go back to sleep so your mind can prepare some welcoming words. Shuni and his brother will not set foot about our tent with the rudeness you showed them."

Mahlah tensed her grip on her cup and then thought better of cracking the baked clay. Shuni's insult still lingered in her thoughts. She was not weak, but she held her tongue instead of rebuking Hoglah.

"What was Mahlah to do? Side with those camel herders over our elder?" Noah capped the milk.

Hoglah stood and brushed crumbs from her robe. "How can you defend our elder after his offense of

151

Jeremiah?"

Noah set the skin against the tent and shrugged. "Jeremiah could not hear the slander. Nemuel wasted his breath."

"You know it all, don't you, Noah." Hoglah kicked at the fire pit and trudged toward the wide path.

"Wait." Mahlah set down her drink and chased after her sister. "You must not leave us in anger."

"Oh, now you speak forcibly, when it is your sister and not a man of Asher." Hoglah wrinkled her nose and tapped her sandal against the dirt.

Her sister would not attract suitors with such an unbecoming scowl.

"I will not speak against a leader of our tribe in public."

"You spoke against him at the assembly."

"I did not speak against him; I spoke for us. There is a difference."

Hoglah halted her foot stomping.

"I promised mother that I would take care of her daughters." Mahlah glanced at her sisters stationed around the fire pit. "We could not have a future together without land."

"I do not need you to take care of me," Hoglah said.

Noah laughed. "I think you do. You ventured outside the camp and brought back a fever."

"Basemath wore the armlet. I did not take a single piece of jewelry." Hoglah held out her hands to show their barrenness. "Besides, why don't you chastise Eli? He was with us."

"I have challenged Eli." Noah finished her drink. "He used fewer words than you, and he showed regret."

"Sisters, enough." Mahlah massaged her temples. "There will be other men who come and seek a wife. May they show us more honor than Shuni and his kin. But know this; I will not be disrespectful to the leaders of our clan. God has placed them in authority, and we will show them the respect they deserve."

"Then Shuni was right about you. You kick a wheel down a hill and stop it halfway." Hoglah marched a few paces toward the outskirts of camp.

Mahlah's muscles tensed at her sister's foolish assessment. *O Lord, soften her heart.*

"Wait," Mahlah called. She was still the firstborn and overseer of their tent. "Take Tirzah with you. Do not walk alone."

"Ah." Tirzah moaned. "My stomach is too full."

"All the better." Noah grabbed Tirzah and tickled her sides. "The manna will not keep until tomorrow. Run and you will be hungry again."

"What about me?" Milcah asked. "Do I have to clean out the fire pit alone?"

"You and I are going to the market to buy some melons. I can provide fruit better than what Shuni brought us." Mahlah picked up an empty satchel. "Noah can clean the cooking courtyard."

"I can?" Noah mumbled with a mouth full of manna.

"We all have to hear words we do not like."

Mahlah grabbed Milcah's hand and headed toward the tents closest to the river. In a foreign market, she could stroll casually among the booths and not bear the burdens of the oldest daughter of Zelophehad.

# 27

The tang of garlic and nutmeg hung in the air surrounding the market. Saliva pooled in Mahlah's mouth. Her jaw tightened from the anticipation of food. She should have grabbed a manna cake before leaving camp. Sauntering among foreign barterers and buyers, she embraced her anonymity. Here among strangers and a few Hebrews, she was not the troublesome woman from Manasseh.

Milcah pointed at a booth resting under the branched shade of a tamarisk tree.

"He has melons." She pulled Mahlah toward the vendor. "Look at the size. Hoglah will soon forget about Shuni's gift."

"It is not the gifts I am worried about." Mahlah dodged around a cart of caged birds. "If only our sister would forget about Shuni."

"Do you not want her to marry?" Milcah stopped at the corner booth and inspected the closest wares.

Mahlah leaned nearer her sister. "She does not have to rush. She has more to offer a man than companionship and children. Our portion of land will be passed down for many generations. When we are dust, the land will still be here."

"Will we have a patch for melons?" Milcah's smile

was all teeth.

"We can grow anything you desire. After our first harvest, we will shout out about our large fruit." Mahlah kissed her sister's forehead. "Now pick a sweet one before we are shoved aside."

Milcah elbowed her way in front of the seller. "Do you have a ripe one for me?"

The merchant scrounged in his coin purse. "My wares are on this wagon. Pick one and be silent."

Before she could draw her sister to another merchant, Milcah fluttered her eyelashes. She let out a breath longer than her thin frame.

"The sweet taste of melon will calm our sister's ills." Milcah pouted at the man.

The merchant cast a glance between her and Milcah.

Not one to feign distress, Mahlah gave a wistful smile. "We came a distance. Surely, there is one better than the others." She rested a hand on her younger sister's shoulder.

"Buy one of these for tomorrow." The merchant thumped the closest melon. "I will sell you another that I keep for my best customers."

Her mouth gaped. This foreigner knew nothing of God's ways.

"I can purchase for today only. Our God provides for tomorrow."

"Hebrews." The man did not hide his disgust.

If she hadn't trudged in the heat of day to secure a peace offering for Hoglah and Tirzah, she would have turned away. She displayed a coin from her satchel. "A Hebrew's coin spends the same as a Moabite's."

The merchant grabbed her money and tossed her a melon.

Instantly, its succulent scent filled the warm air.

Milcah beamed. "I knew he had ripe ones."

"You can carry it then." Thank You, Lord, for small victories. "Shall we head back to camp and slice it."

Nodding, Milcah clutched the melon to her belly.

Mahlah burrowed through the crowd. The swarm of buyers waned as they reached the well-trodden path leading to their camp.

Laughter, taunting yet celebratory, rose above the occasional shout of barterers.

Turning toward the raucous voices, Mahlah recognized Helek and a few of the fighting men from their tribe of Manasseh. Helek strode through the marketplace like a king parading in front of a conquered city. Swords hung from the hips of Helek's kin. She could not glimpse Helek's sword. She saw only his robe. His newly won robe. A robe hemmed in scarlet and purple and adorned with dark forms resembling animals.

Her stomach hollowed as if a breeze off the river whipped through her belly.

"That's the thief's robe." Milcah's fingers tightened around Mahlah's wrist. "It belonged to the bandit who tied up our goat."

"It doesn't belong to him anymore. Helek must have seized it." Mahlah had not told her young sisters details about meeting Balaam in the pit. Memories of the sorcerer chilled her bones. Being this close to his cloak caused her flesh to itch. God's anger at Baal worship had caused the plague that descended upon her clansmen. She remembered Jonah's plump cheeks aflame with fever.

Helek spun around delighting in his newly

acquired garment. His spoil of war was a relic of Baal like Basemath's armlet. Would God send another plague on her people if a robe used to honor a false god was worn into camp?

Her tribesman drew closer. The glee on his face shone brighter than lamplight.

What should she do? Confront a kinsman in public? Keep silent about her knowledge? Her mind cajoled her to flee, but her feet stayed rooted to the soil.

"Sister, it is his robe." Milcah scanned the people hovering nearby. "The thief is not here in the market, is he?"

"He is no threat to us if Helek has his robe." But Balaam and his sorcery were still a threat if she allowed her cousin to enter their camp wearing a pagan priest's garment. She should warn her tribesman so no one else fell ill.

Her mind flooded with doubt. Would Helek believe her story? Her reputation was maligned day and night by the men of the camp. How much more ridicule could her family endure?

Stopping a few paces in front of her, Helek opened his arms in a mock embrace.

"Daughter of Zelophehad, we have acquired more land for you to steal from us."

His companions laughed at his tease.

He thumped his chest. "My robe is finer than a concubine's and certainly finer than yours." Helek swept the drape of his cloak for all to see its adornments. "Your clothing is the color of a branch in the desert. Mine is alive with jewels."

Milcah avoided the sweep of the robe and clung to Mahlah's side.

"Leave us be." Mahlah's voice cracked. A hint of

panic warbled her words. "Do not touch us with that soiled rag. Your prize belonged to a priest of Baal."

"Baal?" Helek echoed. "The man who wore this robe cowered behind women. I beheaded him with one sweep of my sword. He did not wield any power over us."

"We disrobed him before the beheading," his companion said with a smirk. "And after we took his cloak, we disrobed the women."

A few fighting men patted each other on the back. Helek continued to show off his cloak, drawing the attention of more foreigners. Foreigners with no allegiance to her clan, her tribe, or her people.

*God give me strength.*

She wanted to flee the marketplace, race into her tent, and feign sleep, truly she did, but she could not permit a relic associated with Baal to enter her camp. She had seen firsthand the suffering that arose from a pagan armlet.

Clearing her throat, she braced for more ridicule. "Helek, you may think me silly, but you cannot wear that garment into our camp."

"Why?" Helek wrapped the cloth tight to his chest. Black images melded into one beast. "Am I too beautiful?"

Laughter engulfed her.

Helek continued his spectacle of a dance. Onlookers gathered to gawk at the prancing warrior.

"Please, listen to me. We cannot chance another plague on our people." She glanced at her fellow tribesmen hoping at least one would be reasonable. "Those images on your robe are of sacrifices to Baal."

"How do you know that? Did you speak to Moses?" Helek swished his hips as he mocked her.

"Oh, Moses, Helek has a finer robe than mine. Give it to me and my sisters. We are so plain."

The crowd delighted in his rebuke.

Her skin flamed. How dare this fool malign Moses and insult her family. She blew out a breath and rallied her lungs to send forth the truth.

"I saw that robe hang from the body of Balaam, son of Beor."

Hushed whispers rustled through the marketplace at the mention of the priest's name.

"If you do not burn that wicked man's garment, you risk the death of our people." From one face to another, she beheld each of his companions. "Hebrew blood will be on your hands if that spoil of war rests in your tent."

Helek's jaw flared. "Do not tell me what to do, woman." He spat at her face.

She ducked. Spittle dampened the side of her cheek. Her stomach threatened to spill.

"Listen to my sister!" Milcah shouted. Her free hand covering her ear.

"Know your place." Another man spat at Milcah. His saliva hit her chest, narrowly missing their melon.

Mahlah's body became a torch.

"Leave my sister be." Milcah's shriek roared over the heads of her foes. Curious foreigners stepped away widening the circle surrounding her and her tribesmen.

"I stood in the presence of a sorcerer of Baal, and he wore that atrocious rag." Mahlah jabbed at the ornate robe. "If you wear that garment into camp, I will go to Moses, Joshua, Eleazar, and every leader I see, and tell of your misdeed. They will call you before the assembly. All of you." She met each fighting man's thin-lipped frown. "I am speaking the truth as a kinswoman. Death be on your household. Not mine or my clan's."

Helek clawed at her head covering and grabbed a fist of hair. He yanked her forward. "Who are you to demand anything of me?"

Scalp burning, wetness seeped from her eye. She bent her knees and jerked away to release the pressure of her kinsman's hold and to avoid touching one thread of Balaam's cloak.

"Let me go." For a moment, she assessed the knife attached to her belt. Her blade remained useless. Spilling a relative's blood would cost her more than her dignity. It would cost her own life.

Helek laughed at her distress. "Bow to me, and I might forgive your boldness."

She would not go down. Not even on one knee. Not to this foolish mule of a man. Latching onto his smallest finger, she pulled, hard, as if breaking a quail's breast bone.

Her distant cousin howled. He released his grip on her hair and shoved her to the ground.

With the melon as a battering ram, Milcah charged Helek. He fisted his hand to strike.

"Do not harm her." Mahlah lunged and intercepted her sister.

She blocked Milcah from Helek's view. "You may cause me pain, but I will not allow you to harm my sister or to bring suffering upon our people." She beheld every kinsman. "Not after God has given you and our tribesmen victory in battle."

Milcah peeked from behind her. "Does Moses know your names? He knows our names."

A flash of realization caused Helek's companions

to sober.

"My sister speaks the truth. God gave us our inheritance. Perhaps your fathers mentioned our blessing." She challenged her cousin with a fiery-eyed stare and then turned her noble wrath upon his companions. "Moses bestowed our land in an assembly of elders. Surely, Moses would listen to my concerns about a sorcerer's robe when I have seen it worn during Baal worship."

"Do as she says," a fellow fighting man muttered.

Her cousin grabbed his embroidered collar and rubbed his thumbs over a few rubies "Why does this girl wish to take my spoils. God gave me victory over that heathen." Helek wrinkled his fat nose. "She thinks she has the standing of a man."

"I saw that robe on a priest of Baal. In the pit at Peor." If only Balaam's hideous robe could have stayed in the pit.

"We saw the priest on the trail, too," Milcah said. "When our goat was lost."

"If you were in the pit, why do you still live?" Her cousin relaxed his stance.

"I went in search of a relative, not to worship a false god. Please, I don't wish anyone harm. Haven't we seen enough death?" Remembering her father's lifeless body caused pressure to build behind her eyes. "I have told you about the robe and Balaam to prevent more misery."

"Burn it," one of her tribesman said as he strode toward the path home. "I will not accompany that garment into camp."

*Toda raba.*

"God gave us victory over our enemies. I will not stoke his ire," an older fighting man said.

Another tribesman believed her.

Her cousin held out his robe to the objector. "Fine. Burn it then."

The soldier held up his hands. "It is your spoil of war. Not ours. You have worn it. You must place it in the fire and ask forgiveness of any wrongdoing."

"Take it to the fire pits over by the livestock." Mahlah indicated a thin pillar of smoke rising toward the clear afternoon sky. "You will need to wash afterward."

Helek branded her with a haughty glare. "Peck along, old hen. How cunning you were to steal my land. But that was not enough. Now you confiscate my robe." He shrugged out of the tainted garment and let it drag in the dirt. "Woe is the man who binds himself to a thief."

"I. Am. Not. A. Thief." Mahlah's words came out so forcefully, a few women scurried toward the far booths. "God bestowed my father's land on me and my sisters. Moses announced God's law to the tribal elders. We are rightful heirs."

Her cousin spat at the ground, whirled around, and stomped toward the pillar of smoke.

Mahlah's shoulders drooped. The unrelenting heat and the stench of roasted dates caused her head to pound. She rubbed her brow. Why couldn't she have been born the youngest daughter of Zelophehad instead of the oldest?

She rested a hand on the top of Milcah's head.

"Let's go home. I've had my fill of foreigners. And not of melon."

The paths between the tents of her kinsmen bustled with women weaving, cooking, and carting water. A few glimpsed her and Milcah, but no one uttered a greeting. Had word gotten out about the visitors from Asher? Had Helek's companions told tales?

As Mahlah turned onto the wide path leading toward their tent, Hoglah leapt from a sitting stone and raced toward her.

"Mahlah. The tribal elders have summoned us to another assembly."

"Again," Milcah huffed.

Hoglah clasped her hands. A shiver shook her body. "Nemuel's going to try to take our land."

"It can't be so." Mahlah embraced her worried sister. "God gave us our land. No man can take it away." How could the leaders change a revelation from God?

*Oh Lord, may I live one day without turmoil?*

# 28

Family heads of the clans of Gilead, son of Makir, the son of Manasseh, gathered around Moses. Their hand slaps, harried petitions, and foot stomps filled the area in front of the Tent of Meeting. Mahlah's forefather, Joseph, would have been pleased with the boldness they showed in their requests. Hadn't Joseph interpreted dreams for Pharaoh? Leaders from other tribes settled close by, their mouths in furious debate.

Mahlah beheld the shadowing sky. The billowing cloud, the presence of God, consumed the tiptop of the holy tent containing the golden Ark of God. An inner sense of calm overwhelmed her. Never in all her seventeen years had God rescinded a promise. She did not believe He would begin this night.

"What are you thinking?" Noah came alongside, her arms stretched, her fingers intertwined as if she would bolster her sister over the assembly curtain. "I can tell when your eye twitches that you are tense."

"My eye is not twitching." How had it not shut tight with all her ponderings?

"Maybe not but every part of you seems to have been fired in an oven. Would you like me to answer any charges brought against us?"

Shaking her head, Mahlah said, "We haven't done anything wrong. Whatever has upset the leaders of

Manasseh, I will answer for."

Noah raised her eyebrows. "You make me believe there may be accusations against us?"

"Who knows what gossip has tickled their ears. Some days I wish all men were as silent as Jeremiah."

"All maybe, save one." Noah's teasing gaze scanned the assembly. "I don't see Reuben."

"He has yet to return, but he didn't do us much good last time." Mahlah's heart pressed down with disappointment. "If the rumors are true about the battles, five kings of Midian are dead. I would cast a marble that Reuben ventured into that fight. If so, he may be at war or waiting to become clean from the blood he has spilled."

"Shouldn't we approach Moses?" Hoglah pointed to Eleazar, the priest, whose hand was spinning faster than a spindle.

"We prayed last time." Milcah laced her fingers. "All went well."

Mahlah embraced her sister and tugged Tirzah closer. "Bow your heads"

After a moment, Mahlah prayed. "God of Abraham, bless our family. Forgive us if we have done anything to trouble our kin. Give Moses wisdom once again. May the words of our people be pleasing to You."

A chorus of "Hear our plea" came forth.

"Follow me, sisters."

Every sandal flop in her wake reverberated in Mahlah's ears. She secured her mustard-hued head covering and used the cloth to shield herself from the stern-faced stares of her kinsmen. Her stomach tingled like beetles had hatched inside her gut and grazed on her flesh.

She and her sisters, fragranced with citrus oils and adorned in the embroidery of skilled hands, paraded into the sour stench and growling-rumble of men.

Mahlah halted the procession when she was shoulder-to-shoulder with Nemuel on her right, and Abishua on her left. Her sisters formed a barricade behind her.

"My lord." Nemuel bobbed in respect to Moses. "Our Lord commanded you to give the land of our brother Zelophehad to his daughters as an inheritance."

Moses leaned on his staff and acknowledged Mahlah with a nod. "Indeed. It is as you say."

Nemuel stroked his beard. "I have been thinking. What becomes of the land given to Zelophehad's daughters, if they marry outside of our tribe? Would lands designated for our tribe be added to the tribe of their husbands? Upon marriage, the land promised as an inheritance to the tribe of Manasseh would be lost."

Her kinsman, Abishua, stepped forward. "Young men from the tribe of Asher have arrived with gifts for these girls."

Before Mahlah could interrupt and refute the keeping of the mentioned gifts, a leader of the tribe of Asher rushed forward.

"What crime have we committed that you call us by name?" The elder raised his hands, palms open. "Our men passed by the tent and exchanged greetings. That is all."

"Hah," Nemuel scoffed. "Those men did more than saunter by."

Bickering began among the leaders.

Mahlah raised her hand. If only she had a carved staff like Moses.

"I have not received any offer of a betrothal for a daughter of Zelophehad." Her declaration stifled some of the discord. She cleared her throat. "Men from Asher came by our tent with gifts."

Her elders puffed like well-fed roosters.

"Some men were gracious to us on the long march in the desert. They belonged to the tribe of Asher. We were thankful for their kindness. These same men did stop by our tent with gifts, but I returned their wine and food. We have not seen them since."

"Indeed." Nemuel's declaration boomed in the meeting space. "If those men from Asher did return and seek a marriage, they could claim the land of a daughter of Zelophehad. God's provision for Manasseh would decrease. May it never be."

Moses raised his staff.

Discussions halted.

"There is truth in what the elder of Manasseh has spoken. A husband can lay claim to the lands of his wife. Bestowed lands must remain within each tribe. This is what God has ordered. Since our Lord has given land to the daughters of Zelophehad, it is He who must settle this matter." Moses turned toward Eleazar the priest. "I will seek the counsel of God."

After Moses strode beside the holy tent, the elders fixed their snarled-brow attentions upon her.

"See the trouble you have caused?" Nemuel exhaled through clenched teeth. One would have thought he had a snot-filled nose.

She balled her hands and let every harsh word forming on her lips be fisted in her grip. She and her sisters were outnumbered by men who would be elated to seize their land.

"The daughters of Zelophehad know the laws of

God." Mahlah let her praise ring out over the clamoring voices. "We will abide by God's decree tonight and forevermore."

Tirzah tugged on Mahlah's robe. "Does this mean we cannot marry?"

Mahlah stifled a grin and straightened Tirzah's scarlet-hemmed head covering. "It will be a long while for you, little one."

Hoglah shuffled forward. She caressed her shoulder as if it pained. "It won't be long for me. Does Nemuel mean for us to solely marry men from our clan?"

Mahlah let her gaze rest on Noah, then Milcah, then Tirzah, and lastly on Hoglah. Hoglah's eyes brimmed with tears. Mahlah's throat thickened so every word she planned to speak had to be coaxed from her mouth. "We will do what God commands."

# 29

Hand in hand, the daughters of Zelophehad waited for Moses to return to the assembly. What would God decide about the land? Whatever her God willed, she would honor.

Hoglah stood next to her, rigid and paler than her alabaster-trimmed head covering. The half-moons under her eyes rivaled the indigo in her veil.

Mahlah squeezed Hoglah's hand. Her sister's vibrant smile had vanished since the pit.

"Dear sister. God has provided everything we have needed on our journey. Our clothes have not grown threadbare and our sandals are sturdy. We have food every morning and every night. He has not left us alone."

"Then how come I feel downtrodden." Hoglah's hopeful grin faltered.

Mahlah bent to see her sister's face. "We have all suffered the loss of our mother and father, but you are fearful of the loss of someone who made your heart blossom. Try as I may, I cannot heal your hurt."

"I have added to all our woes." Hoglah's voice was but a whisper.

Noah wrapped an arm around Hoglah's shoulders. "You haven't added as much woe as our elders. Besides, your trip to the pit has softened

Basemath's claws. She is bearable of late."

"You are trying to make me forget my transgressions."

"Is it working?" Noah pulled Hoglah into a full embrace.

Tirzah and Milcah shuffled into the circle of sisters.

"We are going to heed the past, but it is nothing compared to our future." Mahlah lifted Hoglah's chin. "God has bestowed on us more than I thought possible. Let us trust in Him."

"Speaking of possibilities." Noah indicated Moses' arrival from beyond the tent.

Mahlah led her sisters in a procession to greet their leader. Elders from her tribe jostled to station themselves near Moses.

Moses shifted his footing with the help of his staff. "Descendants of Joseph. What you have said is true. This is what God commands regarding the daughters of your brother, Zelophehad."

A high-pitch hum filled Mahlah's ears. Silence reigned in the assembly as Moses swiveled to behold her and her sisters. She straightened and encouraged her sisters to do the same with a devout nod.

"Daughters of Zelophehad, you may marry anyone you please—"

*Thanks be to God.*

"As long as your betrothed is from the tribal clan of your father."

The weight of Hoglah's body burrowed down on Mahlah's right side.

Moses scanned the tribal leaders gathered in the front of the crowd.

"No inheritance in Israel shall pass from tribe to

tribe. Every Israelite shall keep the tribal land inherited from his forefathers."

"And what about the other daughters who inherit land?" an elder from the tribe of Simeon asked.

Moses' lips sputtered. "Every daughter who inherits land must marry someone in her father's tribal clan."

"So, it is not just for us," Tirzah asked, careening her neck like a curious turtle.

Mahlah leaned closer to her youngest sister. "God is not punishing us." She willed Hoglah to truly listen to her words. "God is making sure the land He has given to each tribe stays within that same tribe for all generations. And if God has seen fit to provide us with land, He will provide us with suitable husbands."

Noah gave Mahlah a sideways glance. "Maybe we should ask Moses to pray about our husbands."

Hoglah backhanded Noah's arm. "Can't you be serious?"

"I was serious." Noah rubbed her robe. "Life would be so much easier."

Moses thumped his staff. "Daughters of Zelophehad."

Mahlah's sisters startled then stilled.

"This is what the Lord commands of you." Moses let his esteemed gaze settle on each daughter. "You have heard the word of God."

Mahlah stepped forward. "We will do what the Lord commands."

Her sisters came alongside her and bowed. Each one echoed Mahlah's assurance to obey God's command.

Nemuel extricated himself from glee-filled kinsmen and strode toward her family. Beaming, he strutted like a king after a gluttonous feast. "God has protected the inheritance of our tribe. Your father would be proud of your sacrifice."

Warmth flooded Mahlah's cheeks. Heat not from the mass of bodies, but from her elder's arrogance. Where was his compassion for her father when her father wallowed in a widower's grief? Where was Nemuel's restraint when he assessed the visitors at her tent flap? And why did he huddle with the leaders of her tribe when he could have stood with her sisters? She did not need his praise. God's provision soothed her weary bones.

"Sacrifice?" Mahlah repeated with an air of false befuddlement. "If I heard our leader correctly, our allotment of land is secure, and we may choose our own husbands. Husbands that we find pleasing."

"Hmmm." Hoglah tapped a finger to her mouth. "Do you know of any men in our clan who can cook?"

Huffing, Nemuel fixed his annoyance on Mahlah. "Are you going to allow this silliness in an assembly of men?"

"Silliness?" Mahlah shrugged and glimpsed each of her sisters. "My middle sister utters much wisdom. For I can barely bake bread."

# 30

Mahlah wiped her brow as she bent to pick up a water jar. The sun beat upon her head covering, one with a plain brown weave unlike her mother's embroidered veil that she had worn to the assembly. Few women ventured to the well in the heat of the day. All the better for her. She did not wish to hear their remarks about her age, her boldness, and her lack of a betrothal. No man of Manasseh had rushed to her tent with an offer of marriage.

With her sisters in the outlying terrain assisting Noah, her bustling home stood oddly silent. Balancing a jug on her shoulder, she hurried toward the well, making haste past Nemuel's tent.

Wild giggles screeched from the next path over. Those were Jonah's heart-tugging giggles. A woman's voice pleaded with the boy to stop dodging her grasp. Susanna would never catch her grandson. Not after the plague had weakened her body and slowed her gait.

Peeking around the tent lead, Mahlah glimpsed Susanna's stumble-footed pursuit of her grandson.

"What if two women chase you?" Mahlah placed her jar by the side of the tent.

She lunged, arms extended, and nearly caged Jonah.

The boy squealed with delight.

Back and forth, Mahlah leapt until she blocked Jonah's escape toward the wide path.

Short, winded breaths interrupted his laughter.

With one grand maneuver, Mahlah wrapped her arms around Jonah.

"If you have so much vigor, why don't you accompany me to the well?"

"Yes," he giggled.

"Toda raba, Mahlah. I would still be making a fool of myself if you hadn't come along."

Mahlah held onto Jonah until his wiggles ceased. "Go get a cup to bring. You can taste the water before it heats."

Jonah raced toward the tent flap. "Big one."

"A small one," she called out. "You have to carry it."

Susanna drew close, her hand pressed against her chest. "I hear all is as it should be with your inheritance. I am happy God has provided land for your family." She blinked. "I am here for you, for all of you. I cannot say much when my husband is about."

"No one can say much when he is around." Mahlah smiled and clasped Susanna's hand. The scent of hyssop wafting from the woman's skin reminded Mahlah of her mother. Her heart grew heavy like a filled vessel. "You have always been kind to my family."

"Thank you." Susanna squeezed Mahlah's hand. "But I believe it is the other way around. What would we have done without you?"

Jonah jumped from the tent flap, a cup held high over his head. "Rea-dy."

"Have you heard from Reuben?" Mahlah said to Susanna. "Is he outside the camp?" Her belly hollowed at the thought he might not return.

Susanna shook her head. "Some men traveled deeper into Moab to the farthest Midianite cities. Let us hope my son is one of them." Susanna's eyes glistened with tears. "I must hope."

"We all hope and pray for Reuben's return." Mahlah kissed Susanna's tear-streaked cheek. "God will watch over him." As upset as she was with Reuben's betrayal in the first assembly, he had been kind to her in front of Helek and the other warriors. And try as she may not to truly love Reuben, a part of her always would.

Turning from Susanna, Mahlah chuckled at Reuben's son, raising and lowering a clay cup as if it were a jeweled scepter. Her throat grew thick.

"Hurry, Jonah. Before Hoglah returns and finds she has little water."

"You are welcome to take a winding path," Susanna whispered. She plopped on a stool and wiped her brow.

"I will slow my steps." Mahlah winked at her relative.

After settling her water jar on her shoulder, Mahlah ushered Jonah past the tents of the tribe of Benjamin toward the outskirts of camp. The boy sprinted ahead, stopping to urge her onward when he needed a rest.

By the time they reached the well, no one was by the circular wall. Mahlah grabbed the crank to raise the bucket. Jonah slumped against the linen-colored stone and licked his lips.

Mahlah laughed. "You can take the first sip."

She poured water from the bucket into her jar and dipped Jonah's cup.

Puffs of air whooshed from Jonah's nostrils as he gulped the water. His mouth never left the baked clay.

In the distance, someone approached. The form appeared the size of a calf against the mounds of crag-filled hills not far from the Jordan River.

Mahlah squinted. Her heart sped. Could it be Reuben?

As the figure grew closer, she noticed a staff. She recognized the gait and the ornate walking stick. If it couldn't be Reuben, this man was as much a gift.

"Our leader is coming." She tapped Jonah's shoulder. "Let us bring him a drink from your cup."

Leaving her jar by the well, she led Jonah into the shade of a nearby tree. A tree barely surviving, split from a fiery strike of lightning.

Moses met her under the drooping foliage. He leaned against the divided trunk, on the side that lived, where limbs bent away from the charred, decaying branches of death.

"Leader." She bobbed her head. "We brought you a drink."

"Bless you, Daughter." Moses rested his staff on a nub in the bark. "I did not expect to walk so far, but I had to gaze upon her one last time."

Her? Moses' sister had died years ago. What woman would be living in the mountains?

Jonah eyed the height of Moses' staff. He bent and chose a long stick laying in the dirt and then hobbled around the tree.

Mahlah waited for Moses to take a few sips of water. "Did you visit someone in the outskirts?"

Moses' gaze breezed right through her body. She could see her reflection in his eyes, but his mind seemed to be beholding something, or someone, in a vision.

"The land, Mahlah. I surveyed the land." His commanding voice barely uttered its words.

"The land across the river?" She leaned to hear his answer.

"The walls of Jericho are a freshly oiled lamp. You should see the fields and vineyards." Moses' lips curved into a smile. He grinned like a skilled barterer. "The land is ripe for the harvest. Large cities wait to welcome our people. God has blessed us abundantly."

"Praise be to our God. When will you lead us across the Jordan?" Would Reuben return before the journey? She glanced at Jonah who was already digging a new well in the soil.

Moses sipped his water. He stared at the cup. If she did not know him, she would have thought he was ignoring her presence.

"I won't be crossing the river. Joshua, son of Nun, will lead our people into the Promised Land. My body is tired. My brother and sister are gone. I have traveled as far as God has deemed."

Mahlah's mouth gaped. "You are our leader." Her eyes burned. Not from warm gusts of air, or the grit of dirt, but from grief. The grief of losing the only leader she had ever known. A compassionate leader who welcomed her into his assembly with a reserved dignity and bestowed an inheritance upon her family without doubting God's provision.

A prickling heat rushed from her cheeks to her forehead. She blinked back the sting of tears. "I have known none other who talks boldly with our God. How can this be?"

"Do not fret. My heart is at peace with God's decision. Joshua has been at my side for many years.

He is younger and capable of leading our people into battle." Moses reached for his staff. "I know who waits for me. Perhaps I am more ready to leave this land than I let myself believe."

Tears dripped down Mahlah's cheeks. "I will never be ready to see you go."

"No cry, Mah-lah." Jonah embraced her leg, one-armed. He held fast to his stick with his free hand.

"Daughter of Zelophehad, are you not the granddaughter of Hepher, son of Gilead, son of Makir, son of Manasseh?"

Mahlah wiped her cheek and nodded. "Yes." She pressed the affirmation through her thickening throat. How did Moses remember her lineage? Why should her descendants matter to him? "I am from the line of Hepher, a descendant of Manasseh."

Jonah wrinkled his nose at her as if she and Moses had spoken in a foreign tongue. She smoothed the boy's soft curls. His hold on her leg loosened.

Moses cocked his head and lifted his cup in a celebratory manner. "When I speak to God about a woman, I know her name. When I speak to God about a woman and her family, twice, I remember her lineage. The God of Abraham, Isaac, and Jacob knows your name and your lineage. So do I." He drained his cup. "You, my daughter, are destined to venture west, across the Jordan, into a land flowing with milk and honey. But," —he beheld the sag of the branches above his head—"some of the clans of Makir, son of Manasseh, will stay on the east side of the Jordan."

"I don't understand." She wiped wetness from her right eye. With her touch gone, Jonah continued his prodding of the ground with his branch. "Our whole tribe has been waiting to cross the river. To take the land promised by God."

"God has given us victory against the Amorites. Their fertile fields are in our possession. Lands in the east are as blessed as lands in the west." Moses stroked his beard. "Some of your people wish to settle here and raise their flocks. We discussed this at the last assembly. Didn't your elders inform you of their petition?"

Mahlah pondered Moses' words before she spat an unkind remark. She crossed her arms and held them against her stomach. The pressure on her belly reminded her to take small breaths and uphold her position as the firstborn of her family. "I did not hear any new revelations except for who my sisters and I are to marry."

"Of course." Moses laughed with delight like they engaged in lighthearted banter. "How could I forget? The minds of men do not change easily."

Did he think her situation a cause for revelry? Perhaps the heat of the sun had made him giddy? Her hands flexed, but her arm muscles grew taut.

"Oh, Daughter, if your elders only knew how to deal with strong women. I welcomed my sister's challenges. And my wife, she could yell louder at me than at a charging ram."

Moses handed her the cup, but his gaze bestowed upon her an understanding she had not seen in many men. Save Reuben.

"Prepare to cross the Jordan. The elders of the tribes of Gad and Jacob's oldest son, along with the descendants of Makir, have asked to stay on this side of the river. If the men of these tribes cross over and fight for the inheritance of the other tribes, this land will be their home. Look around, Mahlah." Moses opened his arms as if to embrace her. "Soon, you will see these hills no more. You will follow the Ark of our God into the land of Canaan. Your offspring will fill a blessed land."

Tears threatened to spill again but not happy tears. She should feel blessed. At least honored. But the belly beneath her arms held no babe. She had no husband, and her reputation certainly scared away suitors. Even if she crossed into Canaan, she would not fill it with children, not in the near future. Moses spoke as if all the battles on this side of the Jordan had been won and all the fighting men had returned to camp. She waited and prayed for one fighting man to return. And return soon.

"Mah-lah. Look me." Jonah raced around his stick. He had worked the wood deep enough into the ground to make it stand on its own.

A single stick. Standing on its own. Was that to be her future? If that was the life God had prepared her for, then she would see that it was good.

She set the cup on the ground and clapped. "Your father will be happy to see how strong you are getting."

A bitter taste seeped into her mouth. Reuben? Had all the cities of the Amorites been conquered? Had justice been handed out against all the Midianites?

She turned toward Moses. He stood before her as their leader—still. "Have all our men returned from battle. Is this land free from enemies?"

"Our land will never be free from enemies." Moses trudged toward Jonah. "You saw the pit of Peor. Our hearts can be deceived. But not if we hold onto God's Law." He plucked Jonah's stick from the dirt and pointed it at her. "Love the Lord, your God, with all your heart, and with all your soul—"

"And with all my strength." She rested a fist on her chest and felt the pound of her heart.

Moses bowed his head and uttered wisps of words. A prayer. He rubbed the dead branch in his hands. Back and forth the wood rolled until it turned the color of toasted almonds. The tip widened, blooming as if alive. An ornate, beautiful bulb graced the end of the renewed wood.

Jonah giggled and reached for the rejuvenated stick.

"Now you have something to hold onto," Moses said with a wink.

"To-da ra-ba." Jonah jumped in the air, again and again.

Falling face first into the dirt crossed Mahlah's mind, but she stood with a hand to her mouth, soaking in this moment. This very precious moment.

"Crossing the Jordan is not the delight it should be for me." Her lips trembled. "My kinsman has not been heard from since he went into battle, and my heart aches for his son."

Moses retrieved his staff from the tree trunk.

"Remember, Daughter of Zelophehad. The Lord watches over the orphan and the weak. You should not fill yourself with concern." He scanned the distant crags from where he had ventured. "A righteous woman armed with the truth is a frightful opponent. Fear not as you go forth with God." He turned and held her gaze. "Remember, there are always faithful men and women fighting the Lord's battles."

Tears welled in her eyes as a weight lifted from her heart. She nodded with a slight tilt of her head. "Will I see you again?"

Barbara M. Britton

"What do you believe?"

"I will, when my days are through." Her affirmation was but a wisp.

Stamping his staff, Moses said, "Some men still fight north, near Havoth. Take heart, Mahlah. I trust God will give them victory."

*Lord, please let Reuben be one of the men fighting in the north.*

"Stay strong, Daughter of Zelophehad." Moses bobbed his head. The corners of his eyes glistened in the shadows of the split-bark tree. "Joshua will need brave leaders."

"You will always be my leader," Mahlah said, her confession barely audible.

A brief smile flashed across Moses' face. He turned and trudged toward the mountains.

When he strode into the sun, his gray hair sparkled a pure, eye-scorching white.

Mahlah dropped to her knees. "I will go forth with God. Wherever He leads me and my sisters."

Pain swept through her body as if a boulder crushed her bones. The only leader her people had ever known wasn't crossing the river. The man who spoke to God on behalf of her sisters wandered into mounds of dirt and rock. Alone. No, not alone. Their God was with Moses. He had always been.

Jonah ran to her side, hugged her, and rolled his little staff round and round in front of her face.

He was all boy. But a compassionate boy. She grinned at the pride he showed in his smooth, decorated stick.

"Come now, Jonah." She rose and grabbed his dirt-caked hand. "God has given us a new home. We must be ready to cross the Jordan."

Before she retrieved her water jar, she beheld the form of Moses growing smaller among the landscape. She did not recall fear ever revealing itself in his face. He went where God led him. Into a desert. Into battle. Up a mountain. And now, she would go where God led her. Even if she had to cross a raging river with a walled fortress on the other side.

# 31

Nemuel was not at his tent when she left Jonah with Susanna. The grandmother asked a few questions about the small, ornate staff Jonah played with, but Mahlah assured her relative it was a gift, and freely given. She did not know how to explain her encounter with Moses, so she kept her wisdom a secret unto herself.

Mahlah sauntered down the alley south of her own tent. She breathed deep and let her lungs fill to the brim with air that smelled of roasted meat and oak ash. When she reached the wide path, she halted. A camel chewed its cud in front of her cooking courtyard. Tirzah was perched on its hump. Shuni and Hoglah chatted earnestly while Milcah held the large animal's lead.

Why had the man from Asher returned? His insult still branded her memory. 'Not strong enough?' She clenched her teeth. How dare Shuni show himself at her tent after the commotion he had caused by inviting his boisterous kinsmen for a meal. He had to know about the ruling Moses had passed down about her sisters marrying within the tribe of Manasseh. God's words were made known to the elders of every tribe. Especially, the elders of Asher. She and her sisters agreed publicly to marry their own clansmen.

She adjusted her head covering and shifted her blade toward the back of her hip. Nothing, not even a persistent suitor, would keep her sisters from possessing their land.

As she neared the courtyard, Shuni and Hoglah turned and exchanged quick, unsettled glances.

Her jaw slackened. Did Shuni truly believe she was glad to see him? Or were they trying to persuade her to accept a betrothal request? She would not go against God's command. Not now. Not ever.

"Sister." Hoglah stationed herself in front of their guest. She dipped her chin and widened her eyes as if she were a mother about to scold. "We have been given a gift to make our travels easier."

"A gift?" Mahlah surveyed the height of the light-brown camel. Livestock cost Shuni more than a wineskin and some melons. Surely, he knew of the rules surrounding their marriages. Shuni was not kin to her father, nor would he ever be.

"Can we ride him when we cross the river?" Tirzah sat with both legs draped over the same side of the camel's belly. She rubbed the camel's fur with her sandals. "No more bruised toes."

Milcah drew closer, the reins hanging low behind her. "Shuni says we are crossing the river soon. Is it true?"

Well, it appeared Shuni knew some of the latest revelations regarding the tribe of Manasseh. Revelations no one bothered to reveal to her or any of Zelophehad's daughters.

"We are traveling into Canaan. Some descendants of Makir will remain here in the east." Mahlah cast a glance at Shuni. She did not want him to believe he caught her unaware of tribal decisions. *Toda raba,*

*Moses.*

She turned her attention to Milcah. "All of our able tribesmen will fight across the Jordan until our people have taken the land promised to them by God." She turned toward Shuni. "I truly believe the descendants of Asher do not need much assistance in battle. I have never seen a better display of swordsmanship."

Shuni rubbed his chin. "Our sword battles became better known than I would have wished."

And to think, her sisters had witnessed some of their fighting before breakfast. Was he hiding regret? Perhaps, weathering a bit of gossip had brought into her possession a young camel.

He clenched a fist and raised it in the air. "The men of Asher are ready to fight and possess the land of Canaan."

Mahlah patted the bulge of the camel's belly. "We will pray for your well-being and for a swift victory for all our warriors."

Hoglah's eyes were downcast.

"This gift will remind us to be faithful in our petitions for you and your family." Hoglah bobbed her head. A swift dab of her cheek with her veil hid a slow-moving tear.

Shuni snapped his sandals together and gave a brief bow in Hoglah's direction. He turned quickly toward Mahlah as if, already, duty called.

"I would like you to remember the men who offered your sisters assistance on the march to Moab. Not the visitors which angered your kin. May you cast off any insult from my lips."

"God has always provided for me and my sisters, sometimes in mysterious ways." Mahlah pressed her hands together as if in prayer. "I will always remember the men of Asher who showed us kindness. May our God bless you and keep you."

"We can name our camel Asher," Tirzah said with a giggle.

"Alas, that is better than you calling him by my name." Shuni back-stepped toward the wide path. "I am honored to have known the daughters of Zelophehad." His expression sobered. The wrinkles in his forehead made him seem older than his years. "May you travel swift of foot. Shalom."

"Shalom, Shuni," Mahlah answered. "Toda raba for your gift."

Their friend bobbed his turbaned head, turned, and jogged toward the center of camp.

Tirzah cupped a hand over her eyes and watched Shuni's retreat.

"Will we see him on the other side of the Jordan?"

"I hope not." Hoglah shuffled her sandals. "I could not bear to see him with another woman."

Mahlah embraced her middle sister and kissed her forehead.

"You won't have a chance to think of him once we cross the river." Mahlah stroked her sister's cheek. "When our relatives hear we have land and a camel, they will send their sons to fall at your feet."

Hoglah struggled to smile. "Then I will have a basin for washing at the ready." She arched her brows. "For all of us."

# 32

Days later, after traveling from Shittim, Mahlah waited with her sisters a short distance from the bank of the Jordan. The leaders of Israel had given the people three days to bathe and prepare for crossing the river. She and Hoglah could have broken camp and readied their sisters in less than an hour.

Now only nine and a half tribes prepared to travel west. Mahlah shed tears when the women and children from the clan of Makir headed north and east. Her tribe of Manasseh had not separated in forty years. What would her father have thought of the warrior clan's petition to remain in the land of the Amorites? At least the fighting men were crossing the river and going before the masses. Conflicts waited in the land of Canaan.

"I can't see because of all the people." Milcah tightened the lead on the camel bearing the tent. "What are the priests doing?"

Tirzah inched closer to Jonah who sat in front of her on their donkey. "We can only see moving heads."

Mahlah doubted Jonah could see anything taking place on the bank of the river. He snatched at a fly buzzing near the mane of his and Tirzah's mount.

Balancing on a nearby rock, Mahlah craned her neck to see over her leaders' broad forms. Nemuel and

Abishua stood on tiptoe trying to glimpse the entourage hovering near the raging water.

Few dared cross a river at flood stage. If she hadn't heard the stories about God parting the waters of the Red Sea when her ancestors fled Egypt, she would have been hiding under a folded tent instead of gathering young girls to traipse west.

A weak breeze blew the scent of raw fish and damp wood her direction. The fronds on the palms nearest the far shore, swayed back and forth. Was a storm coming? Light gray clouds shielded the sun, but they did not threaten a downpour.

Noah strode past Hoglah and Basemath, a sling hanging from her shoulder to her hip. The muzzle of a newborn lamb chewed on the cloth covering Noah's chest. A distressed ewe followed, bleating her displeasure at Noah's sash.

"Jeremiah, Eli, and I have the herds calmed and ready to move."

Mahlah came down from her stone perch and stroked the lamb's soft fur. "Can the babe not walk?"

Noah shook her head. The mother nudged Noah's thigh. "Its legs are weak. When we get to the other side, I will use this cloth to suspend it from a low-lying branch. His legs should strengthen in time.

A few girls jostled through the crowd. They slowed and giggled at Noah.

"Finally, a birth in the household of Zelophehad."

Noah fluttered her hand at the naysayers. "Do not covet my newborn. I cannot help it is more beautiful than you."

The girls scoffed and scurried away.

"Sister, I am trying to keep our name from among the gossipers," Mahlah said.

Noah shrugged. "They brought up our name, not me." She winked a dark-lashed eye. "I've already endured the flapping hands of a mute over this lamb. Who knew Jeremiah could be so loud."

A hushing sound like an ever-growing hiss fell over the camp.

"What's happening?" Milcah hopped on her sandals attempting to spy the commotion on the bank. The camel tasted its lead and decided to chew its cud instead of the rope.

A cool shiver bathed Mahlah's arms. Soon her family would embark on a journey to claim their inheritance. Land fertile and plentiful awaited them across the river. Someday, her sisters would sleep surrounded by stone. No more transient ramskin dwellings to take down and raise.

She climbed back on her rock and squinted at the water. Forward leading priests supported the gold-covered acacia wood poles of the Ark of the Covenant. They dipped ankle deep into flowing water. On top of the ark, the golden images of cherubim faced each other with wings outstretched and without a care of being carried into the raging current. Why should they fear with God Himself tabernacled between their glittering feathers? "The first priests are in the river." Her voice shrieked with excitement.

A few men shouldering through the crowds balked at her loudness.

"Our God is going before us." Mahlah clasped her hands and rested her chin on her laced fingers.

"Won't they drown?" Tirzah's head whipped around and back so as not to miss a miracle.

"We are following God's command, Little One. Why would He lead us into death?" Her soul filled with joy. "Remember, some of the land on that side of the Jordan is ours. We are going home."

Noah raised her arms. "Praise be to the God of Abraham, Isaac, and Jacob." The newborn squirmed at her words of worship.

The sound of a rushing wind filled the camp. Nothing moved as a *whooo* hummed across the landscape. Her sisters covered their ears, but she scanned the river, bathing in the noise, waiting for God to go before her people.

Murmurings from the crowd, low, yet on a steady rise, masked the eerie howl.

Water flew into the sky as quick as the buck of a horse's head. The light brown, mud-tainted waters retreated, leaving a wide path for her people to cross the river.

Mahlah gasped. Her knees almost buckled.

Noah clutched her arm to steady her from falling off the rock.

Silence fell upon the masses beholding a miracle of God.

She could barely see the harnessed waves in the distance. The Lord had blessed them with ample soil to trod.

The priests' sandals scuffed onto dry land. The Levites traipsed across a river bed with not even a puddle to dampen the dirt. Not a single fish flapped against the solid ground.

"Our God has parted the flood waters. Praise be to our God." Tears streaked her cheeks at the wonder of the One True God.

"I need to see." Tirzah sat taller on the donkey. "I want to see what God is doing."

"Oh, young ones, you will see where the Jordan

ran soon enough. There is a grand passage for all our people to follow." Mahlah bit her lip to keep from wailing with delight. A hint of citrus and bronze flavored her mouth.

Young men raced forward, tugging their ware-packed, wide-bellied donkeys.

Milcah's camel snorted at the interruption. He pulled on his lead giving Milcah's strength a test.

One of the young men attempted to slip through an opening in front of her sisters. A gathering of people surged forward in the young man's wake.

"Oww, my leg" Tirzah cried as women crowded past her mount.

Were these families from the clans of Shemida or Asriel? Why didn't her clansmen from Hepher guard their ground?

Noah pushed at a passerby. "Give our livestock room." Her sudden movement frightened her ewe. The animal burrowed into Noah's legs. Her sister stumbled.

A wave of warmth surged across Mahlah's flesh. If this was how her tribesmen treated her family on this side of the Jordan, how would they regard the daughters of Zelophehad on the distant shore?

Mahlah whipped off her head covering; the embroidered mustard veil her mother cherished. She let it unfurl a few feet and whipped it round and round, over the heads of her sisters. Unsheathing her dagger, she held the blade aloft.

"Halt, you people. Halt in the name of Zelophehad." Her chastisement boomed over the crowd. "My father was the firstborn of Hepher. Respect our place in this line and do not come any closer. Heed my warning, kinsmen of Manasseh. If I witness one more toe stomped upon, I will lash out as an orphan wronged."

The race forward waned, becoming a shuffle of aghast travelers.

Noah swept the spooked ewe into her arm, careful not to bump the newborn. "You heard my sister. Back away." Lunging forward, Noah allowed the distraught mother to bleat at any challengers.

At least Noah's ewe was preferable to her whip being lashed about.

Mahlah's veil swooped over the heads of her sisters like a sling ready to launch rocks.

"We are the clan of Hepher. Do you hear me?"

Nemuel gawked.

Over and over, Jonah chanted, "Heph-r." Tirzah could barely contain him on the donkey.

Basemath, Hoglah, and Susanna banged on wooden bowls.

"Give us room. We are the clan of Hepher," they yelled.

Several families to Mahlah's left started joining in the chant.

"We are the clan of Hepher" rose to a rallying cry. The other clans held back their charge.

Her clan of Hepher plodded forward.

Nemuel and Abishua fingered their beards but kept their mouths closed.

Casting a glance at Jonah all a glee on his mount, Nemuel grinned.

"We are the clan of Hepher," her elder shouted.

Abishua laughed and joined the commotion.

A geyser of giggles sprung from Mahlah's lips. She sheathed her blade and leapt from her stone perch. She waved her head covering side to side and said, "Go

Barbara M. Britton

forth with God."

The remembrance of Moses' instruction cinched around her chest. Oh, how he would have cherished the parting of the Jordan River. The parting of the Red Sea was forty years in the past. Perhaps Moses was watching. Perhaps not. She glimpsed the mountains in the distance and mouthed "Shalom."

Her sisters' heads swiveled all about as their clan trod closer to the dry river. Lush grasses the color of cucumber rind waited on the other side of the river to tickle Mahlah's feet.

*I am walking into a miracle of the One True God.*

The pounding of her heart threatened to flutter her robe as boldly as she had flung her head covering. She sobered at the thought of her God's power.

"Give the priests and the Ark of the Covenant a wide berth," Joshua called to the people. "Do not draw close. If you touch the Ark, you will die."

A few priests walled off the Ark. They stood guard, surrounding the sculpted gold chest—the magnificent dwelling place of their God. Several large rocks hemmed in the Levites.

Were the boulders set by God to protect His people? She would never know, but she appreciated the barrier.

Milcah tugged on the lumbering camel. Her neck craned heavenward catching the faint hint of mist drifting over the parched riverbed. "Will we ever see God dry up a river again?"

"I hope so." Hoglah patted the camel's nose. "And I hope everyone in that walled city is seeing the strength of our God."

"Or hearing about it." Mahlah surveyed the fortress of Jericho as she planted one foot in front of the

194

other where the banished river had flowed. With the mist in the air and the sun overhead, a rainbow shrouded her view of the magnificent city. "I'm sure they have spies hidden in the hills. Truly, Joshua has sent our own spies."

When most of the people had reached the west side of the Jordan, Joshua, son of Nun, sent messengers for all the tribes to send their appointed leader to the banks of the river.

"What are the men going to do," Mahlah asked a messenger.

"Our Lord wants each tribe to carry a stone to our resting place this night. We are to remember God's parting of the water."

"We shall remember. The Lord is our strength and our song. Toda raba."

Tirzah slid from the donkey, carefully so Jonah would not fall. "Did he say the leaders were going to collect rocks?"

Mahlah bent to catch her sister's arm. "The rocks the men are removing from the river will be larger than any in your satchel. Our people shall build a memorial to remind us of God's miracle."

Tirzah puffed out her lip. "Can't I have a small stone? I want to remember, too?"

Susanna approached the donkey. Her eyes sparkled as bright as the hues in the rainbow.

"I will watch over Jonah. Go quickly and find a few for all of us."

Grasping Tirzah's wrist, Mahlah scanned the procession. People still trekked across the banished Jordan, arms raised, mouths open in awe. The crowd thinned near a massive boulder. The natural barricade made backtracking safe, for a moment. Little feet could

Barbara M. Britton

get trampled with oxen and carts on the move to cross into Canaan.

"Hurry." Mahlah reversed her stride and sprinted toward the river. Tirzah gripped her skirt and charged like a skittish goat.

Dodging, sometimes leaping, they made their way to the river bed. The lush foliage on the bushes stood as a testimony to the goodness of this land.

Tirzah reached under the fronds of a fern trampled by frenzied feet.

"Look at this one." She held up a tiny oval of onyx.

"Shhh. Keep your hand low and put the stone in your bag," Mahlah said. "We can't have thousands mulling through the dirt in search of treasures."

"There's a few more under here," Tirzah whispered.

"Ask and it shall be given." Mahlah bent over and helped her sister stand. "Did you get a fist full?"

Tirzah nodded.

Mahlah briefly blocked the procession of clans and angled Tirzah toward their family. The fortress of Jericho loomed over its outlying terraced fields. The hues of green from emerald to malachite to grape leaf contrasted with the sunbaked browns of the desert wilderness.

"Why aren't we going toward the city?" Tirzah clutched her satchel to her breast.

"We are to follow Joshua. Only he and God know when we will attack the city."

Tirzah's brow furrowed. "Won't the people believe in our God after they see this miracle?"

Would the inhabitants of Jericho worship the God of Abraham? Mahlah shifted her head covering into place. What would she have done after seeing a

196

flooded river parted?

"What does our Shema say?"

"To love God with all our heart and soul and strength." Tirzah's voice rang out with no hesitation.

Mahlah's own heart almost burst with pride to hear her sister pronounce Moses' teaching.

"Then I believe if anyone behind those stone walls turns from their idols and believes in the God of Abraham, Isaac, and Jacob, our God will spare their life."

Tirzah cocked her head and smiled. "I believe you, Sister."

"*Tovah*. Good." Mahlah maneuvered Tirzah around two crying toddlers. "Because wherever Joshua leads us this day, we will march."

"More marching?" Tirzah whined.

Mahlah embraced her sister.

"Oh, little one, we will march until we get our inheritance. And now, we are one river closer."

# 33

Hoglah scrubbed an arm across her forehead. "I am ready for a meal."

Mahlah was too, but Joshua led the tribes east, not far from Jericho, but far enough for her to crave a rest.

"At least we are not carrying the large stones from the river."

The sun overhead heated Mahlah's hair like a fiery flame. A grove of oak trees grew as if to touch the shortest ray of light.

"God is showing us another display of His majesty. Look at those grand oaks. I have never seen such stature."

"You are almost as tall as those trees." Milcah laughed from her new perch atop the camel.

Mahlah had taken charge of the beast when it decided Milcah's hair and head covering were best chewed and eaten for food.

Nemuel stalked her direction, hands waving.

"We are camping at Gilgal." He pointed in a southward direction. "We will stake our tents as before between the Benjamites and Ephraimites."

Praise be. She did not know how much farther she could walk without draining their waterskins.

Yawning, Tirzah leaned back on their donkey. "I

thought we were going to live in houses made with stone."

Jonah nuzzled into Tirzah's chest.

"We will have our own dwelling and land soon enough," Mahlah said. "And then I will hear how you are bored and want to travel to search out different stones."

"Not for a long while." Tirzah rested her cheek on Jonah's windswept curls.

Mahlah set their tent not far from Nemuel's, and with the sun drooping almost as fast as her sisters, she left Hoglah to cook the quail that had wandered into camp. Even in Gilgal, God sent provisions for His people. Tirzah and Milcah sat around the fire pit poking at the kindling with sticks. Susanna had claimed her slumbering grandson. Jonah traipsed wearily after his grandmother, still clutching his carved staff.

Mahlah grabbed a water jar.

"I will check on Noah and bring us water from the nearest well."

"Is there one nearby?" Hoglah rotated the spit.

Mahlah opened her arms. "Look around you. This place sprouts grass and blooms like none other I have seen. I trust the farmers that have fled to Jericho will have left their wells uncovered."

"Don't fall in." Hoglah smirked.

"I see your mind is not tired." Mahlah laughed. "I will be back before the meat is charred."

The scent of wet fur rose from the fields on the edge of camp. Herds and flocks trampled land wetter than the desert surrounding Shittim. The air smelled like her tent after a pounding rain.

She spotted Jeremiah stationed by a fir tree.

Alabaster-colored cloth slung from a sturdy lower branch. Noah's newest lamb tried to trot on its legs. The ewe rested not two feet from her babe.

Mahlah shrugged and then swept her hand in an arc. She zigzagged the curves of a woman's body.

"Where is Noah?"

Jeremiah pointed to her water jar and then toward the outskirts of camp.

She guessed her sister had gone to the well.

"You let her go alone?" Plenty of her tribesmen staked tents close by, but this was still foreign land. For the moment.

Jeremiah scowled.

Holding a hand over his eyes, Jeremiah rotated his body as if he was searching for someone.

"No Canaanites are around. They're all afraid?"

He nodded.

"I'd lock myself in that fortress, too. Only our God can control the waters." She trudged in the direction Jeremiah had indicated. "We will need our rest to battle against Jericho."

Why did she even bother to comment? To Jeremiah, she was only moving her lips.

Mahlah quickened her pace as the sky darkened. She stomped past a few cattle and a throng of noisy goats.

"Is the well near," she called to a shepherd boy.

"By the tree." He indicated another oak.

She bobbed her head.

Good. Not far.

As she neared the fawn-brown trunk of the oak, a few ravens shot into the shadowed heavens. A few hovered, flapping their wings and cawing like disgruntled men yelling out questions in the assembly.

Had she disturbed the birds? Had Noah?

The circular stone well stood in the middle of a small clearing. A bucket perched on its ledge while a jar nestled next to its base.

Where was Noah?

Bushes rustled on the far side of the well. Saplings swayed. Twigs snapped.

Had Noah spotted something in the brush?

She squinted into a graying haze.

Noah thrashed at leafy bushes. Was she caught in a vine? Had one of her sheep wandered off? Or was a predator on the prowl?

Mahlah gripped her jar and charged forward with a battering ram made of pottery.

As she grew closer, mudded faces turned her direction. Linen-colored eyes and alabaster teeth glowed amongst the brown, green, and gray shadows.

Tremors wracked her body. These weren't small trees. These were men. Men covered with branches and leaves. Men intent on not being seen. Canaanite men.

Spies.

A deep guttural cry roared from her throat, burning her windpipe.

With her arms tensed, she thrust her jar into the nearest face. Hardened clay struck skull. The vessel's base broke apart. Blood splattered her fragile weapon. One spy crumpled to the grass.

Noah flailed her arm.

Another spy broke from his assault of her sister. His hand lowered and ripped something free from his waist.

She knew that motion. The unsheathing of a blade. She had a knife, too, used it often, but never to slice the flesh of a man. Not even a heathen one.

He was close. Too close. He meant to kill, and she was the closest enemy to slay.

She clutched the shattered jar in front of her chest. "Oh, God of Jacob, be my shield."

# 34

Mahlah's knife was on her hip, not in her hand. Should she attack with her jagged jar? And where should she strike?

The spy shouted. His command came out harsh and battle ready. He sprang, thrusting his weapon upward at her neck.

Pagan!

She raised her pottery piece. His blade chipped the edge, but the force of the blow, cracked her defense. Her clay shield crumbled.

No Canaanite was going to take her life, her inheritance, or her land. Bracing her legs against the soil, she pounced, using her well-marched thigh muscles to focus all her weight upon the spy's knees.

She rammed his legs with her body.

He buckled and slammed against another spy. They both fell.

Prone on the ground, the Canaanite couldn't slice her throat. He would have to stab her and that required a change of hold on the knife's handle.

Mahlah scrambled to her feet. She unsheathed her blade.

"Go! Run Away." She assumed the stance of a fierce warrior, one similar to the men of Asher who battled in her courtyard. She pointed her knife at her twig-covered foe.

Noah, in a stupor, stumbled to Mahlah's side. Blood seeped from Noah's mouth. She reached toward the ground.

"Leave us be." Mahlah slashed her knife at the two Canaanites that remained upright.

*God, I'm claiming Your promise of protection. Now.*

The familiar thud of leather hitting grass emboldened her skittish heart.

Fools. They hadn't taken Noah's whip.

A shout in Hebrew came from the darkness behind the spies. Another warning. Then another.

Two spies darted in the direction of the river.

Mahlah shoulders sagged. She tried to sheath her knife, but the simple motion sent a jarring pain across her body.

Men swaggered through the brush into the small clearing. Fighting men with ridged arms and swords slung on their belts. She recognized their worn leather and strong-jawed faces. Her tribesmen had returned. Praise God.

A commander rushed to the bodies of the fallen Canaanites.

"Spies." Noah indicated the direction the assailants had fled. "They ran toward the river."

A man stalked Mahlah's direction.

She knew those eyes, so fierce, yet caring. A father's eyes. Jonah would be jumping all around his tent.

Reuben grew closer. His beard had filled out. His hair curled at the ends.

She meant to call to him, to her Reuben. But her chest ached, and the ache grew, consuming her thoughts. Her breaths didn't bring enough air. She gasped.

Noah coiled her whip.

"Sister, why are you so still?"

Mahlah couldn't answer. Her response sputtered in her throat.

Slumping to the ground, she held her ribs and prayed for the pain to stop.

Why shouldn't the consuming ache go away? God had answered her prayer earlier. He had sent her a legion of angels. No, he had sent her the fighting men of Israel.

# 35

Noah rushed to Mahlah's side. "What is wrong?" Her cheek bore scarlet streaks of blood from her fight with the spies. She inspected Mahlah's robe. "Did his blade strike you?"

Mahlah breathed in, little by little, trying to fill her lungs to speak. Every puff brought a stab of pain.

"My chest struck that heathen's knee when I dove at his legs." Her lips trembled, but she attempted a smile. Her mouth tasted of grass and river weeds. "If only you had gotten to your whip sooner."

"It was only because of you that I could get to it at all." Noah righted Mahlah's head covering. The cloth had hung like a braid down Mahlah's back.

"Mahlah." Reuben knelt before her. He glanced at their surroundings as if wary of another attack. "What is this about a knife? Were those spies seeking prisoners or sport?"

"Neither." Noah dabbed at her split lip. "I heard something in the bushes. A faint rustle. I thought livestock had wandered off. When I neared where the spies hid, one reached out and grabbed me." She rubbed Mahlah's shoulder. "If my sister did not keep a close watch on us, I would be floating in the river." Tears welled in Noah's eyes. "My brave sister."

"Brave, no. Stubborn, yes." Mahlah winced. "You

would have done the same for me."

She gripped her side and glanced at Reuben. His hair and beard matched the black of the shrouded sky.

"Why is it that I believe both of you would have come to my aid." Reuben's gaze scanned her body, not in a scandalous manner, but as a friend concerned about injury. His breaths puffed like storm winds. "Rest here." He stood and conversed with another warrior.

Mahlah eased toward Noah and rested her forehead against her sister's brow. "We have traveled too far, and we have fought too hard not to receive our inheritance." She struggled to speak. "This land is ours, and I mean to settle it with my sisters. All of them"

"And we will claim our land." Noah grasped her sister's arm.

Bracing a hand against the ground, Mahlah rose.

"Sister, can you carry your water jar." Mahlah took a short breath. "Mine is useless, and I believe we will need to wash."

"I believe after that fright, I could carry ten vessels." With a kiss, Noah headed toward the well.

Jeremiah and the shepherd boy rushed into the clearing. They met Noah by the stone wall.

Mahlah took a few steps and then halted.

"You should rest a while more." Reuben hovered at her side. His beautiful eyes held the same intensity as the night he'd recognized her presence before going off to war. "I could fetch a cart, and you would not have to walk."

She shook her head.

"You should not wait for me. Your family will be overjoyed to see you." She took a few steps and stopped. "One time Jonah saw a man in the desert. He was so happy."

"He thought it was me?"

She grinned. "He thought it was you. He has been watching for your return."

Reuben matched her shortened steps. The glow of the moon sparked a tiny fire in his eyes. "I pray he was not the only one who watched for me."

Her heart rate quickened, sending an ache across her rib cage. She pressed down the hope that lingered in his question, lest she stumble and cause herself more pain. More pain from her injury. Carrying a love for Reuben had always caused her pain. "It was by another well, before we crossed the river, that Jonah and I saw a man walking at a distance." She pushed forward on the path toward camp, joining the fighting men journeying home to their families. Mentioning Moses' appearance would cause more conversation. She kept that revelation to herself. "Jonah and I both thought the traveler was you."

He slowed to a shuffle.

"You thought of me?" His voice held a hint of surprise.

How could he not know? Her blood ran hot. If daylight reigned, her neck would have blushed scarlet. She had thought of him more than she should have, and not only during prayers. "At times, I thought of you."

Reuben stilled. Sheep mulled in the fields. His fellow warriors traipsed toward camp. Rows of tent tops glowed like ghosts in the night, but Reuben did not move. Not toward his home. Not toward anything. Anything, but her.

"There were times I thought of you, too." His broad shoulders and mane of hair loomed over her. He was not much taller than she, but in the starlight, he was a mountain of a man.

She swallowed, but her saliva stuck in her throat like a mouthful of manna. Shaking her head, she rallied her voice. "I don't believe it. Was there talk of my thievery of Helek's cloak? Maybe my forwardness in the assembly." The ache in her chest overwhelmed her entire body. She dipped around his frame. "I am fodder for gossip, not praise."

"I do not believe that foolishness." Reuben stalked beside her. It reminded her of the times when they were children, and he attempted to coerce her to do some task. She usually denied his request, chin upturned, and then did it later anyway.

"Every time I saw new land we had conquered, I thought of you. Every victory brought you to my mind. How you fought for land to carry on your father's name. How you honored God by seeking His wisdom." His passionate speech soothed her like cassia balm.

Was this the same man she sent into battle?

"You speak too highly of me." Her bones grew weary as they passed her flocks. "I think I sought the land out of fear. Fear my sisters would leave me, and I would have nothing." If only her father had not perished. She willed her eyes not to drip tears onto her cheeks. "I want to make a home out of stone and sit on a stool and watch children race around the yard and wheat grow in the fields and watch my flocks graze on a thousand hillsides. Isn't that why we battle for Canaan. For God's gift of land?"

"Yes, Mah—"

"Would you please tell Jeremiah my scratches are not his fault." Noah interrupted their conversation.

Arms crossed against his tunic, Jeremiah tapped his sandal and sulked. The young shepherd boy hovered at his side.

"You did not send her into trouble." Mahlah pointed at Jeremiah and waved sideways. She cut her movement short as discomfort seized her. "My sister cares too much." With a thumb motioned toward Noah, Mahlah placed a hand on her heart and slowly indicated the flocks in the field.

Jeremiah's expression remained stoic.

"I can tend to her tonight." Mahlah reached for the water jar. A twitch of pain radiated across her ribs, and she dropped her arm. "She can attend to the herds in the morning." How on earth would she mimic her words?

Noah feigned being asleep and rested a hand on Mahlah's shoulder.

Jeremiah backed away, nodding his approval. He motioned for the boy to follow.

"Toda raba," Noah whispered, facing away from Jeremiah. She propped the jar on her shoulder. "He was flapping his hands so much I thought he would fly away."

"He cares, sister." Mahlah glanced at Reuben who continued his escort. "Be grateful."

"I am. Most of the time." Her sister marched between Mahlah and Reuben. The clay vessel on her shoulder was a wall forbidding Mahlah to glimpse Reuben's face.

Reuben had thought of her while away warring with the Amorites. Was it true yearning or loneliness for a woman? Any woman.

When they rounded the path toward their tents, excited voices filled the night. Crying. Happy wailing.

Prayers to God.

Nemuel waited outside his tent. Susanna lounged on a stone near the tent flap. A small fire crackled in the cooking pit.

This night, the smoke and ash strangled Mahlah's breaths.

Susanna shrieked when they came into view. "Praise be to our God."

Her friend ran and embraced her son. Nemuel almost hopped the distance to Reuben.

Basemath and Jonah emerged from the tent.

Jonah scrubbed a fist over his eye. He stood motionless.

Surely, he hadn't forgotten his father? Sleep must still shadow his memories.

*Go on, Jonah. Run to your father.*

And as if he had heard Mahlah's silent instruction, Jonah sprinted, chubby legs charging toward his father.

Reuben lifted his son. Holding him high, he laughed, large and boisterous.

"My son, you have grown." Reuben wrapped his arms around his boy like a blanket.

"Did you ever see such a sight?" Noah lowered her jar. "I believe our elder may dance."

"We should all dance. I shall wait some, though." Laughter rippled from her own lips. How could she not enjoy this reunion?

Even though he was held fast in his father's arms, Jonah turned his face toward her.

"Mah." He reached for her, his fist opening and closing.

That was not her full name.

It came again. "Mah."

Pressure built behind her eyes. She could not fight the onslaught of tears. One wet traitor slipped over her lid and trailed down her cheek. She was not Jonah's mother. But oh, how she wished she could be.

She waved her hands to keep Jonah in Reuben's embrace. She ignored the pulse of pain behind her eyes and forced an elated grin.

"Your father is home, Jonah. He wants to spend time with you. I will see you in the morning."

Her sisters spilled from their tent. They glanced from her to Noah. Their noses wrinkled in confusion.

Mahlah sniffed and headed to their tent straight away. She had no greeting. No explanation. Nothing.

Hoglah held the flap open. "What is wrong? You have been gone a while."

From inside the tent, Noah said, "I think she cares too much."

# 36

Sleep did not find Mahlah in the darkness of her tent. Her eyes burned from staring at the tiny bursts of moonlight filtering onto her mat from the stitched seams above. Both her eyes watered. Not solely the right. When was the last time her eye had faltered?

Tirzah nestled on one side of her and Milcah lounged on the other. The heat from their bodies was enough to roast an entire ram. A slight snore gurgled from Milcah's throat.

Noah and Hoglah each slept silently on the other side of the tent.

Mahlah's heart sped at every remembrance of those wicked spies snatching her sister. What would have become of Noah had she not gone in search of the shepherdess? And what had Reuben said about missing her company? Or was it the land he was talking about? Her mind spun with all the events this eve.

A chill bathed Mahlah's arm. She tilted her head. The bruising ache in her chest did not rage as she rolled onto her side.

Tirzah crouched near the tent flap, her ear pressed to the ramskin.

"Is it time to collect manna?" Mahlah squinted harder at the small seam openings.

"Someone's outside the tent." Tirzah's excited whisper caused Hoglah to stir.

"Someone's always outside the tent." Hoglah rolled on her back. "Go to sleep."

"He's pacing," Tirzah said.

Noah opened her eyes. "How do you know it's a he?"

Tirzah crawled closer to her sisters. "I hear the crunch of pebbles."

Was Jeremiah concerned about Noah? He did not want to leave her last night after the attack.

"Maybe it's Jeremiah." Mahlah braced herself and sat. Milcah snuggled closer to her warmth without opening an eye. "He felt responsible for sending Noah alone to the well."

"But I hear mumbling." Tirzah crossed her arms.

This stranger had piqued her sister's interest. The hope of Tirzah rejoining her on the mat was void.

Hoglah blew out a grumbling breath. "There is one way to find out who it is. Open the flap."

Mahlah rose like a withered grandmother and grasped the ties. No one would get anymore sleep if she didn't calm Tirzah's fears.

Tirzah crawled next to Mahlah and gripped her arm. She stared wide-eyed at the opening and stiffened as if ready to pounce on the intruder.

"Noah and I fought off spies, little one." She unlaced the bottom closures. Cool air bathed her covered knees. "I believe we can handle a single man in the middle of the tents of Manasseh."

Mahlah peered out. Her heart spasmed sending a low ache across her ribs.

A man was pacing near the opening. A man she recognized immediately from his swagger and his stature.

"Reuben?"

What was he doing outside her tent?

Tirzah crowded her face cheek-to-cheek with Mahlah's between the flaps.

"Did you bring any gifts?" Tirzah giggled. "We are fond of melons."

# 37

Mahlah scrambled to her feet. She stood barefoot in the dirt facing the man she had dreamed about for years. The soil was cooler, softer than she realized, but she would not leave to gather her sandals. She had taken root in his presence. Her nerves had her heart at an all-out gallop, so much so, her cheeks pulsed with every beat. They should not be out in the dark alone. Well, with the eyes of Tirzah bearing down like a hawk on Reuben's every shuffle, they had an ever-alert chaperone.

"Is something wrong?" It had to be. What other reason could there be for him to seek her out in the dark of night? She licked her lips and waited. Her mind flung random thoughts on the mischievous breeze.

Reuben rubbed his jaw and stepped closer. His eyes sparkled under the ample moon. He glanced toward the tent flap.

The opening to her tent was cluttered with amused and curious faces.

Chastising her sisters to go inside would stir whining and protests. Their grinning lips were at least closed. So much for sleeping.

"I didn't get to finish what I was saying earlier." He cast a glance at her sisters. "I tried to put it off until morning, but I am too restless."

What had he said? She envisioned their walk back to camp. He had thought of her. And Jonah. He had thought of the land. Did he wish to stay east? Settle in the land of the Amorites?

"I missed you." He slid his fingers down the hair framing her face. One slip and she would feel his touch on her lips. "More than I should have." His confession rumbled deep in his chest and caught in his throat. "I have not noticed what has been right in front of me."

The sweep of his hand, rough, yet gentle as a morning dove, sent a wave rising in her belly. She should push him away, but she leaned closer to feel his breath and not miss a single word from his mouth.

This couldn't be happening. Not in front of the tent she had staked since a girl. Why now? Why not before when he accepted another woman as his wife? The ache in her ribs couldn't compare to the ache that consumed her when Reuben had taken a wife into his tent.

"Were you lonely at war?" That had to be the reason he came to her with such a burning need. Her lips trembled. His thumb was but a hair-width from her mouth, still, yet waiting.

"I was." His gaze held hers. "Lonely to be a father to Jonah. Lonely, in wanting to be a husband again."

And she was an easy match. A woman older than most and with land bestowed. A double-portion of land since her father was the firstborn of Hepher. But she had responsibilities to her family, to her sisters. She couldn't leave them alone.

He tipped her chin. "You are too quiet. The woman I know would be telling me all that happened while I was away. Before she fought off spies."

His freshly bathed scent swept her toward the stars. "I am in a daze."

His strong-jaw smile mesmerized her. "Let me wake you." He caressed her cheek. "Be my wife. Lay beside me when I return from fighting. Allow me to comfort you when others slander your good name. I will defend you like I have before and challenge any man who dares utter your name with contempt."

Tears welled in her eyes. "I have waited so long." She touched his hand and withdrew it from her skin. "I have thought of you every day since you left." Her heart struggled to beat through her grief. Wetness flooded her cheeks. "But now I fear it may be too late. I promised my mother that I would take care of my sisters. I cannot ask you to take on my responsibilities." No matter how she tried to stop the flow of tears and be the straight-backed, broad-shouldered eldest daughter, she failed. "I am the firstborn of my father."

"I know. I have lived alongside the daughters of Zelophehad all my life." He wiped the tears clinging to her chin. "Be with me, Mahlah."

The stars in the night sky blurred through her tears. How could she leave her sisters with a fortress looming on the horizon and warring nations all around?

She cast a glance at her sisters. She knew everything about them. The wave of their hair. Every amber hue in their eyes. When one would bicker, and another would fall silent. She opened her mouth, but her voice fled.

"I need a moment with my sister." Noah stomped from the tent. She waggled her eyebrows at Reuben. "I am sorry to interrupt again. Wait here and do not move."

Noah pushed Mahlah into the tent. Her sisters jumped backward, parting like the River Jordan.

"Why are you standing there like a mute," Noah asked. "I would have leapt into his arms by now."

Tirzah chuckled as she closed the tent flap.

"Do not heed Noah's advice, little one." Pressing a hand to her chest, she turned toward Noah. "I promised our mother I would take care of you. How can I leave you now in this new land?"

Noah shook her disheveled ringlets. "Where do you think we are going? We have lived down the path from Reuben all of our lives. Besides, Hoglah can manage our tent."

"I have been feeding you for more than two years now." Hoglah rubbed Mahlah's shoulder. "There have been few complaints."

"Save your own." Noah smirked.

"Why don't we set up three tents?" Milcah stretched her arms toward the tip of the tent. "You and Reuben can live between his family and ours. When he is off fighting, you can sneak and sleep with us."

"With Jonah," Tirzah added, leaning on Mahlah's hip.

"You cannot be around every one of us all the time." Noah cupped Mahlah's face. "God has watched over us. The One True God will not forsake us. You have taught us that, and you believe it to be true."

"I do." Fresh tears threatened to spill. She adored the touch of her sister's slightly calloused hands.

"You cannot refuse this offer of marriage because of us." Noah squeezed Mahlah's cheeks. "I won't let you."

"And if someone asks for my hand or Noah's?" Hoglah swatted their shepherdess. "I will send Tirzah

Barbara M. Britton

and Milcah into your tent to sleep."

Mahlah held out her arms for her sisters to gather. She embraced their warmth and breathed in the soft scent of myrtle from their skin. The ache in her side engulfed her whole body.

"You are always welcome in my tent," Mahlah whispered.

Noah eased away. "We have our land and each other. Nothing will ever change that."

"No. Nothing will ever change that." Mahlah gazed into each of her sister's eyes. "Ever."

Milcah blew out a shuddered breath. "We will go forth with God."

Moses had challenged Mahlah with those same words. She smiled through quivering lips.

"And nothing will ever change that."

"Then what are you waiting for?" Noah flung open the tent flap.

Reuben consumed the entrance to her tent. Her Reuben. His eyes glistened in the moonlight. The boy she had chased over hill upon hill was now chasing her and desiring to be her husband. Her heart soared to the highest star.

"I've heard everything through the ramskin. An extra tent can be arranged. And more tents as our family grows, for I will fight for you and your sisters to inherit all your father's land." He arched a brow and when his gaze met hers, it could have set a sparrow to sing. "And if it pleases my future sisters-in-law, I would like to enter your tent." His lips curved, harnessing a grin. "There are some things that need to be done in private."

# 38

Mahlah's knees almost gave way as Reuben strode toward her. This had to be a dream. Her bones became weightless as a feather. The smallest puff could have sent her wafting toward the heavens.

"Reuben? You are entering a tent of unmarried women. Is this wise?"

"I've been waiting many days to give you a kiss." His gaze captivated her as he drew closer. "Shall I do it on the path and stir more gossip?"

"It is dark outside," she mumbled.

"It is dark in here." He tipped her chin.

Shushed giggles filled the shadowed night.

"Sisters, face the side of the tent."

On tiptoe, she pressed her lips to his and then tried to pull away. His strong arms held her to his chest. He deepened their kiss. Her body awakened as if from a long trumpet blast. All the years of loving him were made right in this simple expression of his love.

Whatever the future held for her, she would face it with her God and her family. Her new family. Her growing family.

She broke his kiss and settled on her feet, her hand covering her lips. The touch of him still lingered. Forceful, yet smooth and gentle.

She glanced at her sisters' darkened forms and met the twinkle of eyes.

"When did you turn around?"

A shuffling sound at the tent flap interrupted her reprimand.

Jonah crawled into the tent.

"Me, too." Hands raised, he opened and closed his fingers.

Reuben lifted his son and kissed his cheek.

"All this kissing," Milcah huffed.

"Jonah, come back here." Susanna followed her grandson through the flap. "Oh." She stifled a grin. "Is the asking over?"

Basemath joined her mother. "She must have agreed if he's inside their tent."

Noah stepped forward. Her breath tickled Mahlah's ear. "We definitely need three tents. I'm not sharing a tent with Basemath."

Nemuel entered. Everyone shifted farther from the opening. "The way this family is growing, we'll need to conquer a small city for land."

"No grum-ling." Jonah leaned his head on his father's shoulder.

Mahlah pressed her lips together and glanced at Reuben.

He laughed.

She laughed.

The giggling in the tent disrupted the calm of the night. Even Nemuel grabbed his belly and joined in the raucous laughter.

Reuben, her betrothed, leaned forward to sneak another kiss.

Jonah leaned in, too.

All their cheeks met in the middle.

Joy filled her being. *Toda raba, Adonai.*

How blessed to be going forth into the Promised Land with God, a husband, a son, and the daughters of Zelophehad.

# A Note from Barbara

I wish I had discovered the story of the daughters of Zelophehad many years ago, especially when I taught elementary school chapel. I don't know how I missed the bravery of these orphaned girls during my read-through-the-Bible sessions. Perhaps it's because they are first mentioned in lists of names—not the most exciting reading material. Mahlah, Noah, Hoglah, Milcah and Tirzah first appear in Numbers 26:33 and Numbers 27:1-11. You will find the restrictions put on their marriages in Numbers 36. They are also found in Joshua 17:3-6. They are not one hit wonders in Scripture.

I admit, I was leery of writing a story with five characters even though Mahlah is center stage in this book. I hope each daughter touched your heart with their courage to change history. Their petition to inherit their father's land was a bold ask of a male-dominated assembly. Since they were not married, they could have been younger than the ages of my characters. We don't know how Zelophehad or his wife died. I thought the snakes in Numbers 21 would be an exciting and moving exit for Zelophehad.

God takes care of the orphan and the widow (Exodus 22:22-23). He watched over Zelophehad's daughters and blessed them, and other women, with the gift of land. I am so excited to bring the story of these wonderful girls to light.

Thank you for reading my story which is really God's story. The daughters of Zelophehad continue with *Heavenly Lights: Noah's Journey* and *Claiming Canaan: Milcah's Journey*.

May you go forth with God.

*A Sneak Peek at*
*Heavenly Lights: Noah's Journey*

# 1

*Every good and perfect gift is from above, coming down from the Father of the heavenly lights, who does not change like shifting shadows. ~ James 1:17*

### The camp at Gilgal
### In the Promised Land of Canaan
### Near the fortress of Jericho

Noah *bat* Zelophehad tugged her donkey farther from the ramskin tents of her tribe of Manasseh and farther from the stone fortress of Jericho. In the distance, the walls of the Canaanite city rose up, up, up, above the lush plain. How would the army of Israel lay siege to a barricaded city? No one had gone in or come out of Jericho for several Sabbaths. If any of her tribesmen dared to draw near the gates, they would be struck with arrows and rock. Boiling oil awaited warriors who neared the city of the false moon god.

The sooner Jericho fell, the sooner she and her sisters would inherit their father's land. Land where she could watch over her herds and flocks without the oversight of her kinsmen.

Noah squinted in the midday sun. From the hill outside of camp, priests carried the gold-covered Ark of her God, the God of Abraham, Isaac, and Jacob. The glistening seat of her God was hemmed in by warriors from the tribes of Israel. Was this their seventh trip around the pagan city? Seven. God had promised their leader Joshua a victory in battle after the seventh lap on the seventh day. *Adonai* honored all His promises. When this city of idols fell, all the people in Canaan would know her God was the One True God. And her God had bestowed a portion of this land on the daughters of Zelophehad. Five orphaned sisters who dared to ask for a forbidden inheritance.

A long, eerie howl echoed from the priests' ram horn trumpets. The hum vibrated across her skin like a shiver. Soon, with one long blast that battle horn would call her people to war.

Did the Canaanites not realize it was futile to battle a living God? Surely, the watchmen stationed on Jericho's wall had seen her God separate the waters of the River Jordan. Her people had walked across a flooded river on dry ground. Shouldn't the Canaanites have believed in a blink? They must be blind to miracles. Or they were fools?

She stroked her donkey's damp neck. "At least our fighting men have plenty to drink thanks to your strong back. Now it is time to satisfy your thirst." She led the donkey up a slight incline. Her arms burned from filling waterskins since before dawn.

*Nooooaaaah.* A young goat trotted in her direction. The kid butted her leg with his nubby horns.

"I have no milk for you. Where is your mother?" She gently guided the kid toward the herds of resting livestock." Sheep, goats, and cattle slept in small clusters, forming mounds on the landscape for as far as she could see.

"You are wasting your time with that one." Enid, a young shepherd boy, rose from the shade of a tall oak.

"That goat has bothered me all day."

"Did he nurse?" She scanned the scattered livestock for the pesky goat's mother.

"Yes." Enid motioned toward a boulder. "His mother rests behind the rock."

"*Tovah*. Good. He is an unblemished firstborn." She rubbed the kid's head with her free hand. "Where is Jeremiah?"

Enid cocked his head toward the north. "With the breeding camel. She is laboring"

Heat surged through her body. "We have waited over a year for this birth."

"Go." He indicated the walled city and took hold of the donkey's lead. "I'd rather watch God punish Jericho than gaze upon a bloody calf."

Turning, she noticed the last of the rear guard rounding the east end of Jericho. *Oooh Ahhh.* Another ram's horn blast announced the progression of the fighting men of Israel. Her people were gathered at the edge of camp, nearest the city, waiting to shout when the army completed their final trip. Her sisters' screams would represent the family of Zelophehad well.

*Nooooaaaah.* The persistent kid butted her ankle once more.

"Your mother has food for you, not I."

Urging the young goat toward the boulder where its mother rested, she backed away slowly, and then sprinted to where the camels bedded. Her whip bumped against her hip.

In the cool shade of an acacia tree, a camel lay on its side, ankles bound, lest the animal assault Jeremiah with her hooves. Other camels foraged for grass as if this were any other day. If they only knew that after this birth, they would witness the annihilation of a fortress.

Jeremiah knelt under the shade-giving branches, hunched near the rump of the camel. The mother's grunts and head rears did not distract him from his duty. He would hear neither Noah's calls, the slap of her sandals, nor the trumpet wail. The shrieks of the Canaanites and their judgment would be but a breeze upon his cheek. Perhaps today was not a bad day to be deaf and mute.

As she drew closer, a waft of blood and urine filled her nostrils. Her eyes watered. The air smelled like a slaughter.

She waved her arms to gain her fellow shepherd's attention.

He glanced at her, but in his eyes, the usual glisten of light brown sparks had disappeared.

On the ground, the calf's front legs and head were visible. Hazy, white film covered the babe. The mother craned her neck and snorted. Her calf's head jostled forward but did not shift farther out of the womb. Was the calf stuck?

Kneeling by her fellow shepherd, Noah brushed the thin shield of skin from the babe's nose. The wet sheet clung to her hand. She stretched out her arms and motioned a pull. Her thumb indicated she would be the one to finish the birth. Surely, Jeremiah could see her arms were slighter than a man's and would easily slip into the womb. Would he accept her help or be stubborn?

Jeremiah's brow furrowed, his arms wrapped tight around the babe. He hesitated and tugged once more. Huffing, he released his hold and nodded toward the camel.

She grabbed the castoff birthing and rubbed it on her arms. Her stomach wretched at the feel and stench of the fluid. The sun's heat did not help the odor either. The sour taste of grain sizzled on her tongue, tightening her jaw.

Staring at her, the babe's brownish-black eyes beheld her as if she were its only hope.

"God is the giver of life. Not me." She brushed the soaked calf's head with her fingers and slipped her hands in the camel's womb. The mother attempted to kick. She mouthed a short prayer. "It will be over soon," she said to the anxious camel. Hopefully, she spoke the truth.

Slickened fur warmed her fingers as she slid her hand down the bone of the babe's back legs. A tiny hoof had burst through the birthing skin. The bend of one knee had wedged against womb and bone. As if peeling a lemon, she released the leg from the thick rind of its mother's muscle. Praise be, the womb had not ruptured.

The mother bucked its head. Jeremiah lunged and comforted his beast.

With a gentle pull, the calf sprung free and slid over Noah's knees, soiling her robe. She would need a good soak in the river to clean her garment. She removed her arms from the womb and helped Jeremiah clean the whitish sack off the calf's body. He whisked the babe to a waiting bed of straw.

New life had been birthed into the herds of the clan of Hepher. She struggled to her feet.

A gush of water and blood drained from the camel and flooded Noah's sandals. Warmth seeped around her toes.

Truly a dip in the Jordan awaited.

"Sorry about my arms." She patted the mother's rump.

Taking a small knife from her belt, she cut the mother's bindings and hopped away from the hooves. The mother stumbled to her feet and plodded after her newborn.

Sweat trickled down the side of Noah's face. She glanced at her soiled hands. Where was the washing jar? Next to the oak. She hurried to clean herself.

A long trumpet howl blasted from the direction of camp and from the direction of Jericho. Before the horn hum ended, an ear-splitting shout rose from her people in obedience to God's instructions.

Beneath her sandals, the ground quaked. The stone wall of Jericho, solid and forbidding, collapsed in a cloud of white dust.

Her knees trembled. The God of Abraham, Isaac, and Jacob was here fighting for her people—His people—as He had promised.

"Praise Go—" Her heart beat filled her throat.

A second plume of dust drifted toward her, covering the landscape in a haze. The dirt storm traveled to greet her and Jeremiah and the newborn camel. This plume was not from crumbled stone. Herds stampeded from the direction of the fallen fortress, eyes bulging, nostrils flared. Shouting a warning would be useless for Jeremiah. His ears could not hear her words.

Spooked hooves charged closer.

Her skin tingled as if the dust were fiery embers.

She needed cover. In the open fields, there was no escape from a stampede of crazed animals.

*Nooooaaaah.*

# 2

Jeremiah *ben* Abishua scrubbed a hand over the tiny camel's head as its hooves rustled a bed of straw. He wished to comfort the newborn with a voice he did not have. *Why Adonai? Why have you caged my speech like a fang-toothed panther? Do I not understand most of what is spoken from the lips of others? My mind is able even if my ears are worthless save to itch in the rain.*

He glanced through the branches of the acacia tree and blinked at the sunlight. *You know my heart, Lord. Uncage me if for a day. Is it a sin to desire to be worthy in the eyes of men? In the eyes of one woman? Can't I do something noble to bring honor to my father's name besides birth a camel?* His brow furrowed. Even Noah had helped with that.

The stone barricade around Jericho loomed far from the fields. His brothers marched somewhere in the mass of men waiting to attack the city and bestow God's wrath. Warriors younger than he were allowed to fight the Canaanites while his own strength was ignored. God had promised a victory, so why couldn't he bring honor to his family in battle? His older brothers had grown wise and muscular over the years as he, too, filled his height with muscle. Yet, while now they would never challenge him to wrestle, they still treated him like a weak, unweaned child.

The babe's mouth opened as its mother licked its head. The odor of straw and wet fur filled the air under the acacia tree. He should reassure the mother camel and keep her calm, but he had no words to speak. Why couldn't he shout, "Blessed are we that Noah has thin arms."

Noah.

His chest burst to sing her name to the heavens and to sing praises to his father, Abishua, and to her eldest sister, Mahlah. Was he even worthy to ask for a betrothal? Would children from his loins be as silent as he? He scrubbed a hand through his hair. Could he bear to pass on such a burden?

The mother camel nuzzled her babe's head. The newborn scrambled to rise from the straw. Did it need to nurse?

His sandals slid as though he walked on pebbles. Had he been in the heat too long? No, he'd birthed the calf in the shade. The earth was moving under his leather soles.

Jericho? The wall.

He turned to see if the city still stood. A storm of dust covered where the fortress wall had loomed. The haze clouded the air near the outskirts of camp. Had the wind surged? His mouth gaped and filled with grit.

Livestock charged the tree line.

He grabbed the newborn camel and set it behind the tree trunk. The mother followed without a slap.

Picking up his wooden shepherd's staff, he lunged and whipped the long piece of wood in front of his position. *Whoosh. Whack.* His father's camels would not be trampled. Nor would he. *Whack.* With all his commotion, animals scattered. He would retrieve them later with—

Noah! He glimpsed her in the flatlands near the large rock.

Inside his head, he imagined her lively, smiling face. His lips parted, but he could not call to warn his shepherdess. He didn't even know the sounds to make.

*Whack*! One arm flapping like a startled crow, the other wielding his narrow-hooked staff, he raced into the chaos. The pound of his heart reverberated in his dead ears. If only the pounding inside his chest was loud enough to scare the closest beast.

Pushing frightened sheep out of his way, he coughed as dust filled his nostrils. He spat dirt from his mouth and hastened onward. He had to save the woman who made life worth living.

He had to save Noah.

*We hope you enjoyed this snippet from the next book in the Tribes of Israel, Daughters of Zelophehad series. Look for the trilogy wherever books are sold.*

*A Devotional Moment*

Why should our father's name disappear
from his clan because he had no son? Give
us property among our father's relatives. ~
Numbers 27:4

---

One of the hardest tasks Christians have to do
is to discern when to "buck the system." We're
instructed to submit to authority as long as laws
don't contradict God. We work at our jobs, pay
our taxes, drive under the speed limit—obey all
laws—even if we feel they are unjust. Taking on
our government in protest of a law is often
difficult and can cause great upheaval in our
families, our circle of friends and even our
community. But occasionally, it is time to take a
stand. So we go before lawgivers to demand a
right, knowing that the answer might be "no", but
hoping that if we present our case fairly, the
answer will be "yes." Speaking in front of others is
sometimes a great fear, but if the cause is
sufficient, we can, indeed, "buck the system."

In **Lioness: Mahlah's Journey**, five young
women in a patriarchal society must stand before
the law-giver and ask for what is theirs, despite
decrees saying otherwise. Their faith sustains
them as they present their case. Trusting God, they

approach with humility for the Lord's favor.

---

*Have you ever felt paralyzed to take a stand? Perhaps unfairness affected you directly; perhaps it was something that affected a friend, coworker or even an entire community. What did you end up doing? When we know it's time to stand for what's right, the best thing we can do is to pray for the wisdom to know what to say and do, and for the strength to persevere whatever firestorm might arise. Fear is an emotion we can overcome with positive action—even when we're shaking in our proverbial boots.*

---

LORD, TEACH ME TO SEE INJUSTICE, TO STAND IN FAITH AGAINST WRONGFUL LAWS THAT CAN HURT OTHERS AND GRANT ME THE WISDOM TO KNOW EXACTLY WHAT TO SAY AND DO. IN JESUS' NAME I PRAY, AMEN.

*Thank you…*

for purchasing this Harbourlight title. For other
inspirational stories, please visit our on-line bookstore
at www.pelicanbookgroup.com.

For questions or more information, contact us at
customer@pelicanbookgroup.com.

Harbourlight Books
*The Beacon in Christian Fiction*™
an imprint of Pelican Book Group
www.pelicanbookgroup.com

Connect with Us
www.facebook.com/Pelicanbookgroup
www.twitter.com/pelicanbookgrp

To receive news and specials, subscribe to our bulletin
http://pelink.us/bulletin

May God's glory shine through
this inspirational work of fiction.

AMDG

# You Can Help!

At Pelican Book Group it is our mission to entertain readers with fiction that uplifts the Gospel. It is our privilege to spend time with you awhile as you read our stories.

We believe you can help us to bring Christ into the lives of people across the globe. And you don't have to open your wallet or even leave your house!

Here are 3 simple things you can do to help us bring illuminating fiction™ to people everywhere.

1) If you enjoyed this book, write a positive review. Post it at online retailers and websites where readers gather. And share your review with us at reviews@pelicanbookgroup.com (this does give us permission to reprint your review in whole or in part.)

2) If you enjoyed this book, recommend it to a friend in person, at a book club or on social media.

3) If you have suggestions on how we can improve or expand our selection, let us know. We value your opinion. Use the contact form on our web site or e-mail us at customer@pelicanbookgroup.com

## God Can Help!

Are you in need? The Almighty can do great things for you. Holy is His Name! He has mercy in every generation. He can lift up the lowly and accomplish all things. Reach out today.

*Do not fear: I am with you; do not be anxious: I am your God. I will strengthen you, I will help you, I will uphold you with my victorious right hand.*

~Isaiah 41:10 (NAB)

We pray daily, and we especially pray for everyone connected to Pelican Book Group—that includes you! If you have a specific need, we welcome the opportunity to pray for you. Share your needs or praise reports at http://pelink.us/pray4us

## Free eBook Offer

We're looking for booklovers like you to partner with us! Join our team of influencers today and periodically receive free eBooks!

For more information
Visit http://pelicanbookgroup.com/booklovers


## How About Free Audiobooks?

We're looking for audiobook lovers, too! Partner with us as an audiobook lover and periodically receive free audiobooks!

For more information
Visit
http://pelicanbookgroup.com/booklovers/freeaudio.html

or e-mail
booklovers@pelicanbookgroup.com